Show, Don't Tell

DRAMA!

The Four Dorothys

Everyone's a Critic

Show, Don't Tell

Don't miss the next show!

Entrances and Exits

DRAMA!

Show, Don't Tell

Paul Ruditis

Simon Pulse

NEW YORK   LONDON   TORONTO   SYDNEY

SIMON PULSE

An imprint of Simon & Schuster Children's Publishing Division
1230 Avenue of the Americas, New York, NY 10020
Copyright © 2008 by Paul Ruditis
All rights reserved, including the right of reproduction in whole
or in part in any form.
SIMON PULSE and colophon are registered trademarks
of Simon & Schuster, Inc.
Designed by Mike Rosamilia
The text of this book was set in Weiss.
Manufactured in the United States of America
First Simon Pulse edition April 2008
2 4 6 8 10 9 7 5 3
Library of Congress Control Number 2008922272
ISBN-13: 978-1-4169-5905-2
ISBN-10: 1-4169-5905-X

☆ For Chris ☆

Mamma Mia!

"Where did *those* come from?"

"Bryan!"

"What?"

"Stop it!"

"I'm just saying . . . I always knew you had breasts there, but they've never been so *there* before. It's . . . disturbing."

"I swear, one of these days I'm going to kill you."

"So long as you don't smother me."

That was the point I got smacked in the head.

Okay, let me back up and explain. The Renaissance Faire had come to town. For those of you reading those words and groaning right now, I am *so* with you. Dressing up and staying in character all day with the "thees" and the "thous?" That's too out there even for *this* Drama Geek.

But for those of you who maybe did a little bounce in your seat and got all aflutter over the idea of lords and ladies in ye olde tyme clothes, speaking ye olde tyme language, while eating ye olde tyme foodstuffs . . . you should talk to my best friend Sam. You have *loads* in common with her. Sam grew up traveling the country with the Renaissance Faire every summer until that fateful year she started at our high school and entered, stage right, into my life.

Prior to my getting smacked, Sam had come out of her bedroom dressed in one of her Renaissance Faire costumes. Even though I'd seen them hanging in the closet loads of times, it was an entirely different experience seeing it on her body. The long green skirt that swept to the floor and the somewhat sheer, somewhat low cut, white, short-sleeved blouse were nice enough. But the real problem was the blue bodice she wore on top of the blouse. The small vest was tied—tightly—in the front. That act shifted what God had given her up front farther up and way farther out, making her breasts appear five times their normal size.

Seeing as how I lived in Malibu and she was in Santa Monica, we'd spent plenty of time at the beach together. I'd certainly seen Sam in bathing suits before, but this was an entirely different experience. Not to say that Sam is totally flat or anything. But this was ridiculous. You could use those things as a bookshelf to stock the entire line of Shakespeare's plays . . . and still have room for some Christopher Marlowe texts as well. There was nothing but naked flesh from the bottom of her chin to the top of her bustline, and it was, quite frankly, a little unnerving.

"If Sam's freaking you out, wait till you see me," my other

best friend, Hope, yelled from Sam's bedroom. "But I think I'm going to need some more help first. Sam?"

"Coming," Sam said as she disappeared back into her room. The grunting began mere seconds later.

Whatever was happening in there, I was certain that I wasn't prepared for it. Hope's chest is *way* ample to begin with. No telling what the end result would be. To spend the entire day with the two of them at a Renaissance Faire dressed as the boobsey twins was going to make this all the more fun.

And by fun, I mean miserable.

Before the movie in your mind starts costuming me in pantaloons, let me stop you at the opening credits. I'd agreed to go along to the Renaissance Faire because it was important to Sam that I see a bit of her other life and meet her oldest friends. Renaissance Faire living was not a lifestyle choice I would ever make for myself, and there was only so far I was willing to go for friendship. As such, I was wearing a pair of black shorts that went down past my slightly pale knees and a short-sleeve, button-down shirt with my usual fedora topping off the ensemble. No olde tyme clothes for me, thank you very much.

Okay, the fedora was kind of old, but at least it was from this century.

"What is with this torture device?" Hope's voice carried throughout the apartment.

"Just shut up and exhale," Sam replied.

Though I was dreading the day of Renaissance whimsy that lay ahead, I was loving that the three of us were together again. Hope had just gotten back from six weeks visiting her mom in New York. This was the first time our trio was reunited. Just in time for some last-weekend-of-summer fun. School was set to start on Tuesday, so this was our only chance for one crazy weekend before the structured doldrums of Orion Academy beckoned.

Even better, Sam's boyfriend—and my former foe—Eric, wasn't coming back until Monday. Like Hope, Eric had spent the summer on the East Coast with his mom and her life partner, Claire. He'd briefly returned to town the weekend before, then jetted off for a weeklong vacation with his dad. This meant that Sam was all ours before going back to full-time coupledom. And we were going to make the best of the time we had left. We had it all planned: Ren Faire days and Hollywood nights. And by Hollywood nights, I don't mean we were going into that tourist trap to party like rock stars. We were going to be renting movies and dishing about our plans for senior year of high school.

I know. We're wild.

"Ready?" Hope asked from Sam's bedroom.

"Not even," I said, bracing myself.

Hope stepped out into the hall and walked into the living room. It took all that I had not to react. My jaw was fighting to drop. My eyes were bursting to bug out. My heart was even beating in the rhythm of a bubblegum pop dance hit. Her outfit was simple enough: black from top to bottom, including a black hat with a green feather. But it was the bodice on the outfit that really made her . . . stand out?

Hope isn't exactly shy about the girls. She jokes about the size of her breasts all the time. Normally, we play along. But there are times when I know that the joke is not going to be appreciated at all. And this? Was *so* one of those times.

"Get it over with," she said, resigned to the comments she was expecting from me.

I held my tongue till it hurt. I was biting down to keep that tongue from saying anything my brain was too smart to let past my lips.

"Really. It's okay," she said. "I know I look rather . . . endowed in this thing."

Understatement of the *decade*! If you could use Sam's chest as a bookshelf, I'd say you could land a 747 on Hope's. "No," I lied. "It's . . ."

Crickets.

Yeah. I couldn't come up with anything.

"Here, Hope, try this," Sam's mom, Anne, said as she came out of her room with a long emerald green piece of fabric that could have been a cape. I couldn't say at the time, because my mind was seeing nothing but bursts of colors as my brain refused to process what was before me. It was one thing to see my best friends on display, it was quite another to see my second mom and favorite teacher so . . . *gah!*

My face went shades of red that do not exist in nature. I focused on the floor so fast I think I gave myself whiplash. "My eyes! My eyes!"

"Bryan, grow up. They're breasts," Anne said. "All women have them."

"I'm sure we have some tights around here that would look darling on you," Sam offered.

"Thanks," I replied, "but I left my codpiece in my other pants."

Once I could refocus, I saw that Hope looked much more demure with the green cape pinned at the base of her neck. She'd probably get warm as the day went on, but at least she was decent.

"No, leave the hat," Anne said. "It works."

Hope froze in a state of minor uncertainty halfway to ditching her hat on the coffee table. She calls her personal wardrobe style "Goth-Ick," which translates into all black outfits with one splash of color. That's pretty much all Hope wears, whether for day-to-day or on special occasions. With the green cape and matching feathered hat, she was working two whole colors. They were the same color, true, but we could all tell that she was having trouble justifying an ensemble that went against her signature fashion.

"You'll probably have to take the cape off at some point." Sam said what I'd been thinking. "So you'll be down to one color eventually."

"Fine," Hope said, as she put the hat back on her head. A green cape and a green feathered hat was more color than I had seen on Hope in a long, long time. I *had* to get a picture.

"Paparazzi time," I said, reaching into one of the many pockets in my shorts.

"Go-Go Gadget Shorts!" Sam cheered as I searched for the camera. These were my favorite shorts because they had so many pockets for me to hide things in. The downside was that I could never remember what pockets I put anything in.

I finally found my thin digital camera in the zippered pocket on my right thigh and directed the costumed trio to line up along the wall. They all struck wild poses ranging from the proper and poised to the bold and bawdy in their period costumes. After about a half dozen shots, we were off to the Renaissance Faire.

The excitement in Anne's car was palpable, just not my palp. At eight-thirty in the morning, it was way too early on a summer day to be up and about. Sure, I could have met them at the faire, since it was halfway between Sam's apartment and my house, but going together was half the fun. I could sleep in once school started back up. Besides, I wasn't so sure that a Renaissance Faire was something I wanted to face on my own. Being a Drama Geek was one thing, but Ren Faire Geeks were a whole 'nother level of eccentric. I mean, they have their own language.

For years before Sam and I met, she and Anne would go on the Renaissance Faire circuit during their summer vacations. They would travel from town to town across the country from the end of June until the beginning of September, living in a traveling city of campers like modern-day gypsies. Being that it was a Renaissance Faire, they dressed like gypsies too. All that stopped the first year that Sam participated in the Summer Theatrical Program at our school, Orion Academy. I guess if you want to do the Ren Faire circuit, you have to sign on at the start of summer or the caravan leaves without you.

Those gypsies can be surprisingly militant.

But Sam and Anne still keep in touch with their gypsy friends who tour the world year-round in all their Renaissance Faire glory. I missed out on meeting everyone the year before because my family vacation happened to coincide with the weekend the faire was in town. But this year, my folks and I went away earlier, the faire came later, and now I got to experience the entire thing in its full Renaissance glory.

Oh, goody.

It was just after nine when we turned off the main road and pulled into the long, winding entrance to the Adamson Country Club. As we passed the sun-faded sign, Hope caught my eye and we both started laughing. Uncontrollably.

"Stop it," Sam said through clenched teeth, without looking back at us.

"Sorry," we said, like siblings being chastised by our parents on a long car trip.

"It was the only space available for rent," she explained to us *again*. "Labor Day weekend gets booked up early around here."

"Naturally," we replied.

"It's perfectly normal for a Renaissance Faire to have sand traps," I said, forcing a straight face. Which was tough to do considering neither my face nor any other part of my body was straight in the least.

"Oh, shut up," Sam said, as we entered the parking lot.

I'd been to the Adamson Country Club a bunch of times growing up because my Grandpa Willie was a member. When he passed, my grandma let the membership lapse. The country club itself lapsed soon after. Not that the two events were related. Though many of my grandparents' old friends had come up to me randomly on the streets of Malibu over the years to say how the place hadn't been half as fun after they'd gone. And that they blame my grandparents for it closing.

Only half of them seemed like they were joking.

Donald Trump had recently bought the abandoned country club and was planning to convert it into an even more garish display of wealth. The redesign was supposed to be so massive that the city was making him jump through a bunch of hoops to get the proper permits. Never a man to let any investment go to waste, he was renting out the grounds for all kinds of events since he didn't have to worry about the greens being torn up. Which is why the golf course was now covered in multicolored tents with flags rising way higher than the little red ones in the holes ever got.

Once we finally got to the parking lot, I was surprised to see how empty it was. This did not bode well for the faire on opening day, I thought. Little did I realize that it mostly didn't bode well for me.

"Where are we going?" I asked as Anne bypassed spots near the entrance. A small collection of people were gathered on the grass, playing music and dancing in front of the gates that still seemed closed from my vantage point in the car. Anne, however, drove to the far end of the lot, past the main building where there was a second collection of cars and some more dressed-up people.

"Performers' entrance," Sam explained. "Since we're help-ing Marq and his folks at their shop, we don't have to pay to get in."

"Always a plus," I said. It was one thing to have to spend my last weekend of summer at a Renaissance Faire. It was quite another to be expected to pay for the experience.

"I can't wait for you guys to meet Marq," Sam said as we got out of the car. "He is just . . . too much to be believed."

"Can't wait," I said, though I totally could. I'd been hearing about her GBF for years. (*Aside:* GBF stands for "Gay Best Friend." I didn't take this personally since Sam and I had never discussed the G in my BF status. Not that it was something I was hiding. It had just never come up in conversation. Quite frankly, I'm not all that big on putting a G before the BF any-way. I don't go around calling Sam my "Straight Best Friend." I prefer to think of us as BFs without any qualifiers.)

Marq and Sam used to be summer friends growing up. During that time, they spent every day together on tour until school started and Sam returned to Santa Monica and Marq headed home to Gainesville, Florida. His family had gone full-time Ren Faire for the past year, taking the world tour through the winter and spring. Sam was particularly excited to see him and hear all about what he'd been up to.

I was slightly more wary about this reunion as it was the first time the two platonic men in her life were about to meet. I'd had a nagging sense of dread about this all morning as I counted the many ways that the new friendship dynamic could blow up in all our faces. It's never easy meeting your

BF's GBF, especially when she doesn't know that you're her GBF as well.

We walked up to the back entrance where a somewhat large, considerably round man was seated on a bench. He wore an abusively beaming smile plastered on his face beneath a bulbous red nose and surrounded by a bushy beard with flowers woven into the whiskers. I think they were daisies.

"Good morrow, fair wenches," he said with a lecherous growl directed at Anne and Sam, who were in the lead. I suspected he'd already been dipping into the mead that morning before I even smelled his breath.

My eyes flitted to Hope, who bore no trace of a reaction on her face to being called a "wench" so early in the morning. Sam had prepped her in the car to make sure she knew that "wench" wasn't an insult. It wouldn't have been a good start to the faire experience for Hope to knock the greeter to the ground on his ample ass before we even got inside.

"On what business do you seek entrance to yon merriment?" The man's head nodded back to the fairgrounds on *yon*.

"We are merchants engaged by the House of Sandoval," Anne replied in character with a bit of an accent I'd never heard before, which was . . . odd.

"Ah, a fine and noble establishment," he bellowed, checking his clipboard. "Prithee, names?"

"Mistress Anne Lawson," she replied with a polite nod of her head. "My daughter, Samantha and her young cousins, Hope and Bryan." Sam didn't even react to the use of her full name, which she usually hates. I guess in the Renaissance world, she doesn't find it as annoying. I wasn't quite sure why Anne was passing Hope and me off as relatives, but I didn't say anything.

The guy checked our names off the list as he checked us out. He stopped at me with a bit of a scowl. "And what of this layabout lout?" he asked in what I can pretty much assume was not a term of endearment. (*Aside:* Sam has since confirmed this for me. "Layabout" and "lout" pretty much meant back then what they mean now. She helped me with some of the other terms too. I stuck them in the back of the book for anyone who might be following along.)

"He dresses in an ill manner," the man continued. "All those seeking entrance prior to the festivities must be properly adorned."

As far as I was concerned, I looked pretty darn proper in my clothes, but the costumed people all around me didn't seem to agree. Particularly those bunching up behind us in line. "I can go around the front and pay to get in if it's a problem," I said to Anne. Tickets only cost fifteen dollars. It really wasn't worth any drama.

"The faire doesn't open for an hour," Sam said.

Which would explain why the lot had been mostly empty.

Much as I didn't want to sit out in the parking lot alone that long, it seemed like a better option to me. I already felt like the proverbial sore thumb sticking out. The previously jovial guard had a pronounced scowl on his face as he regarded me like *I* was the one dressed like a freak.

"No," Anne said, more to the guard than to me. "Bryan, the faire has always been a welcome place for *everyone*. You are a guest of the House of Sandoval. That should be enough for entrance."

"If that be the case," surly said, "then a representative from the House of Sandoval must be sought. No entrance will be permit until such time."

Sam let out an exaggerated sigh. "I'll go get someone," she said as she huffed past him.

But she never had the chance.

A high-pitched *squeeeeee* rang out through the fairgrounds, scaring all manner of dog in the vicinity. Seriously. There was barking and everything.

A flash of white and gold ran toward us as an ornately dressed girl morphed her squeal into an "OhmyGod-OhmyGodOhmyGod!!" And topped it off with a "SAMMY!"

I barely made it out of the way before she plowed into Sam, wrapping my friend up in layers of an elegant dress that were somewhat out of place among the wenches with me. The "OhmyGods" resumed as the newcomer bounced up and down with Sam joining the girl in her squeals.

I wasn't sure who this girl was, but it seemed odd to me that Sam had never mentioned her. It isn't just anyone who can get a squeal out of Sam. Scratch that. I don't know *any* person who has ever gotten Sam to make that kind of noise. And the bouncing up and down in excitement was also new.

"You look *fabulous!*" the girl said as she planted a big kiss right on Sam's lips before releasing her. "Your boobs finally grew into that dress! Not that I ever . . . oh my *GOD*, it's the motherload of breasts. You must be Hope!" The newcomer released Sam and directed her attention to Hope, saying, "I must press myself up against those things." And then she did, planting a surprising kiss right onto Hope's lips.

"Marq!" Sam said, giving a playful slap. "You're worse than Bryan."

Marq?

"Bryan?" Marq asked at the same moment I realized that it was a boy under that layer of white powdered makeup, matching white wig, and tons of gold dress. "Bryan from Orion? Is he here?" He turned to face me. "As I live and breathe—in spite of this corset. This *must* be the boy I've heard so much about."

I took a step back for safety. Marq was kind of overwhelming. And it had nothing to do with the fact that he was dressed rather literally like a drag queen. Everything about him was times ten. Not to mention that his effeminate manner made me look positively butch in comparison, which—considering I use phrases like "positively butch"—is saying something.

"Bryan, meet Marq," Sam said with a laugh.

"Hi," I said, tensing.

Marq leapt toward me. I quickly thrust my hand out between us so that he couldn't molest me like he did my friends, forcing him to skid to a halt. His body language reacted like I was holding a gun on him. Once he realized my hand wasn't loaded, he daintily took it between his thumb and two fingers and gave me a genteel, ladylike shake.

All in all, I preferred it to a kiss on the lips.

"I feel like we're old friends already," Marq said as his genteel shake turned into a tight squeeze and he pulled me into a reluctant hug. I managed to avoid the kiss as he released me. He didn't even bother to hide that he was giving me the once-over, looking me up and down like the contestants on *Project Runway* drool over a bolt of way-too-expensive fabric that would look perfect draped over one of their models . . . or themselves.

By the time his eyes completed their journey back up to mine, my entire body tensed like it had during the hug. I didn't like what I was seeing in those eyes. There was a lot of suspicion mixed in with a dash of excitement. It was when he added the half smile with a nod that freaked me out more than his wardrobe.

There was no doubt what was going on in his mind.

He knew.

A Connecticut Yankee

I'd met people with highly developed gaydar before, but this was *insane*. How could he possibly know that I was gay from a quick "Hi" and a hug? I'd hardly even hugged back.

But Marq knew all right. I could see it in his eyes. It was right there beside the look that told me he wanted me to know that he knew. And maybe that he might suddenly want everyone else to know that he knew.

I didn't know how I felt about that.

I wasn't in the mood for someone to pull a Perez Hilton and out me against my will. And I certainly wasn't ready for it to happen at the Renaissance Faire.

Not that coming out was something I was afraid of doing. It's just that I'd never seen much point in it. I wasn't dating anyone, so what did it matter whether I liked boys or girls? Sam didn't tell me she was straight before she started dating her current boyfriend, Eric. Come to think of it, she never told me she was straight afterward either. She just let the whole "dating a boy" thing be the major clue. I'd always figured that I'd let people take that as a clue for me . . . whenever I found a guy who wanted to date me, that is.

Still working on that one.

Grumbling from the people gathered behind us indicated that we weren't exactly making new friends holding everyone up from getting into the faire. That blessed grumbling distracted Marq enough to take his eyes off me and turn to Sam. Okay, it wasn't so much the *grumbling* as the guy in back who yelled, "God a mercy, get this queue moving!" But I'm not going to quibble.

"Come on, my parents are dying to see you all," Marq said as he started his way into the faire.

"Your most gracious Majesty," the guy at the gate said to Marq as if it was perfectly normal for the queen to be a queen. Which, maybe, it was. "This knave—"

"Petey, save it for the tourists," Marq said, snapping a lace fan open and waving it in front of his face. "Speak modern."

"The kid isn't wearing a costume," the guy—Petey—said with a sneer in my direction. "You know the rules. No costume, no entrance. He's got to pay like the rest of the rabble."

Marq snapped the fan back shut and smacked the guy on the shoulder with it. "Petey, what kind of store do my parents run?"

"A costume shop," Petey said.

"A clothing emporium," Marq corrected. "Don't you think that maybe he'll be getting outfitted there? I mean, it's not like you can just buy this stuff on the streets of Hollywood." He punctuated his statement by swirling his dress at Petey. "Well, maybe you can in Hollywood, but he lives in Malibu."

I didn't think that it would be the best time to correct Marq's misconception about my costume plans, or lack thereof. But I did wonder just how much Sam had told him about me. No surprise that he knew I lived in Malibu, but there was something in the way he spoke that sounded like he was way more familiar with me than I was with him. Or maybe he only *wanted* to be more familiar. Either way, I guess what he was saying worked—or Petey was just sick of us—because he waved us by to the relief of those lined up behind us.

Anne thanked Marq once we were inside, while Sam asked the question that was definitely on my mind. "So," she said to Marq, "what's with the dress?"

"You like?" he asked, giving a twirl that sent the hem riding up several inches. I, for one, was glad that it stopped before it reached his bloomers. "That hagseed, Jocelyn, is up for the part of a dead body in one of those medical dramas about angsty doctors in love. She's got an audition this morning. Since I'm her understudy, that means I get to be the queen today."

"She's going to miss the opening day of the faire for an audition?" Sam asked in a scandalized tone, like she wouldn't have done exactly the same thing for a chance at a bit part on a TV show.

"I know!" Marq said, bouncing up and down again. "But I can't really blame the beast if it means I get to wear this pretty, pretty dress and greet all the guests like the queen I was born to be!"

I guess Sam caught the questioning glance between Hope and me. "Jocelyn plays Queen Elizabeth. She sits inside the front entrance waving to the people as they come in while her servants attend her. It's a position of honor in the faire hierarchy. You have to be here awhile to earn it. Usually it goes to one of the kids raised on the faire."

"It helps to have parents high in the faire administration to strong-arm the other founders into voting you in," Marq added in a loud voice that made me suspect there were founders in the vicinity. Hope and I nodded our heads in understanding. Living in Malibu, we understood the politics of daddy power. "Course, it would've gone to Sammy if she'd stayed on the circuit. Not only does everybody here love her, but Anne has chopped off more heads than the whole French Revolution. Combined."

"It's nice to know my reputation still holds," Anne said, lightly. This was a side of my favorite teacher that I'd never seen at school. It was, I might add, rather scary considering I was going to have her for English when school started on Tuesday.

"Speaking of medical dramas," Hope added. "I heard the evil stepsisters talking about Holly auditioning for a dead body too. Maybe they're up for the same part." She was referring to Holly Mayflower, a classmate of ours that we tended to refer to as the bane of our existence.

"Let us pray to the god Dionysus that she gets it," Sam said reverently, bowing her head.

"You do realize that they won't *actually* kill her," I said.

"I guess," Sam said, with a note of disappointment. Then she perked up. "But starting school Holly-free for a week would be almost worth listening to her brag about the part for the rest of the year."

"*Almost*," Hope and I said together.

"As a mother and a teacher, I hear none of this," Anne said, holding her hands over her ears as we strolled through the waking Renaissance Faire.

She couldn't hold those hands up for long. People were coming out of the woodwork to welcome her and "Samantha" back, grabbing their hands for a shake or pulling them into hugs and kisses. Lots of kisses with these faire people. Especially from the ones with signs hanging round their necks that said HUG ME. That was a little too friendly for me. Especially when they came up and pulled me into hugs before I'd even been introduced to them. I am a major believer in personal space.

It was overwhelming, all the hands and arms that came at us with shouts of "Good morrows" and plenty of celebratory "Huzzahs!" thrown in. With all those people rushing up to Anne and Sam to exchange greetings and get hugs, I felt like I was walking with faire royalty.

Considering how Marq was dressed, I guess we kind of were with royalty. And though they treated the queen with due respect, everyone was running up to say "Well met!" to Anne and Sam. It was the most welcome I'd ever felt anywhere in my life, though I did catch a few people eyeing me questioningly, which I'm going to assume had something to do with my lack of costume. Have to admit, I kind of did stand out a bit as the only person in the entire place not in period garb.

Marq, however, still seemed to be eyeing me for an entirely different reason that I tried my best to ignore.

Most people didn't stay long to chat. They were busy setting up to start the first day of the faire. All around us, carts were coming to life as the faire people prepared to hock their wares. It seems that a Renaissance Faire, in addition to being an exploration of an earlier time, is also one big flea market, with people selling things from jewelry to weaponry and everything in between. There was even a booth with those massage chairs set up like you see in the malls. An anachronism, for sure, but I suspect many of the men who are forced to come by their wives and girlfriends wouldn't mind spending a couple bucks getting a "kneading from a lightskirt."

We passed a food court in the center of the faire, already open and offering breakfast treats like steak on a stake, Scotch eggs, funnel cakes, and pickles sold straight out of a barrel, which I found to be kind of random. The mix of scents coming from the fried foods was making my stomach grumble. I'd gotten up so late that I hadn't even had time for a Pop-Tart. I assumed we'd have time for snacks later. Marq didn't even slow down as we made our way past and he filled us in on all the local gossip.

"Oooh, ooh, ooh," he said as we passed a soothsayer's tent. "Scandeliciousness! You remember Mistress Catherine of the

Tarot, right?" Sam nodded eagerly. "At our Vegas stop, she was arrested for public indecency for being naked in the park at midnight. She claims it's religious persecution because she was just communing with the Goddess. But that doesn't explain what Goodman Folcroft was doing there butt naked too. Lord knows, he doesn't follow the Goddess."

"I'm guessing Goodwife Folcroft would like an explanation for that too," Sam said with glee.

"Huzzah!" a shout went up as a huge maypole was raised in front of us.

"That's the first time I've ever seen the maypole up before the gates opened," Anne said. "Is it possible that after twenty years people are finally starting to get their acts together?"

"What stands the hour?!" Marq suddenly burst out, scaring us all.

I looked to Sam for an explanation on that one. "What time is it?" she asked.

Oh.

Since I was the only one wearing a modern timepiece, I told him it was almost nine-thirty.

"Fie," he squealed. "Don't want to be late. It's time to show these peasants a real queen!" He wrapped Sam up in another bouncing hug. "You *have* to come by and see me play the part. Oh, and meet Drea! She's on dungeon duty. I am so thrilled you're here! Mom and Dad are at the end of the row. Primo spot next to the Tournament Arena." And with that last stream of consciousness burst, he flounced off toward the front entrance.

There was a moment of silence in his wake.

"So far as I know, he's the first guy ever to play Queen Elizabeth," Sam eventually said.

"That's quite an honor," Hope said, though I wasn't sure if she was being serious.

Watching Marq flit away in a very unmasculine manner, I kind of felt like that particular milestone was still safe. All I know is that I was glad he was gone. Every time he gave me that look I felt both dirty *and* afraid. Figures the first time a guy my age ever cruised me, he was dressed like a girl.

"Attend, my fine lad and lasses," Anne said with a clap. "The House of Sandoval awaits!" She stormed off, in character, with her long skirt billowing around her.

"She missed this, didn't she?" I asked Sam.

"We both did," Sam replied as we hastened to follow.

The House of Sandoval was at the back end of the fairgrounds. Best I could tell, there were four long rows of booths, carts, and tents that people could wind up and down as they toured the place. The food court was dead center, but the other big draw had to be the makeshift arena at the back of the place. A sign by the arena's main entrance listed a series of tournaments that would take place at various times over the course of the day. This was where the jousting and the sword fights and the stunt shows would occur.

Right beside the entrance to the arena was a collection of large canopies all tied together. Under those canopies were more costumes in one place than any other setup we'd passed since coming in the side entrance. From the purposeful stride both Anne and Sam were taking in that direction, I could tell it was our destination.

The big wooden sign with the words HOUSE OF SANDOVAL painted on it was a subtle hint as well.

"Anne!" a high-pitched voice squealed as a woman—this time, an actual woman of the female persuasion with curves and everything—came running toward us, wrapping Anne up in a big hug. This, as it turned out, was Marq's mom, Rowanne Sandoval. She asked us to call her Sandy.

Sandy was a big, boisterous woman who sucked us all into tight, smothering hugs with the kind of familiarity that would make you think she'd watched Hope and me grow up alongside Sam. (Sorry, *Samantha.*) Sandy was exactly the kind of person who would give birth to a child like Marq, I suppose. Wearing what I assumed was one of the finest frocks from the House of Sandoval, I couldn't help but notice that there was something different about how she filled out her dress than my friends did.

I wasn't the only one who noticed.

"Wait a minute," Hope said, checking Sandy out. "How come she looks like she does, and I look like I do?"

"Now that you mention it," Sandy threw the green cape back behind Hope's shoulders to get a better look at the landing strip, then turned to Anne. "How could you put this girl in that outfit?" She wrapped an arm around Hope and pulled her toward the tent. "This is the problem with small-chested women. They simply don't understand what it's like to be graced with something extra. God a mercy. Come with me."

Sandy led us into her tent and started loading Hope down with outfits.

"She only wears black," Anne said.

"With a splash of color," Sam added.

Sandy gave them a sideways glance, grabbed the clothing out of Hope's hands and dropped them on a table, then piled on anew with costumes the color of night without skipping a beat. During the process, she told us to say hi to her husband, Daniel. I hadn't even realized there was anyone else in the room.

Sitting in a corner, going over some paperwork, was a quiet, bald little man who merely squeaked out what sounded like "Hello" in response. He too was exactly the type of person I would imagine to be the father to Marq and the husband to Sandy. Families have a way of balancing out. With such bold personalities in the mom and son positions, it was to be expected that dad would disappear into the background.

"Those should do you fine for a start," Sandy said once the pile in Hope's arms went over her head. "And don't you worry about paying. You can work off the cost by helping us out."

"That's okay," Hope said from behind the pile in a muffled voice. "I've got my credit card." Considering she didn't have a purse or any pockets, I was wondering where she was keeping it.

"Nonsense," Sandy said, but Anne held up a hand to stop her. Hope could easily buy out the entire stock, but that wasn't why Anne was stepping in. Hope was very sensitive about taking freebies. Being the daughter of one of the top entertainment lawyers in Los Angeles certainly had its perks. Her stepsisters wielded the Rivera name freely to get them swag wherever they went, even though they could more than afford it. That made Hope so angry that she went out of her way not to abuse her father's position and bank account.

Sandy didn't seem to understand, but she didn't say anything either. She just pointed Hope in the direction of the curtained-off dressing rooms and then turned to me. "And now, I've got some breeches that will help camouflage those pale, skinny, little legs of yours." She grabbed me and started taking my measurements with her hands.

"I'm fine," I said, pulling away. "I'm good. Just fine. I'm going to stand over here."

Sandy looked to Anne, who just shrugged. "Oh, I'll be getting him into costume before we leave next week," Sandy said, slipping back into character. "On that, I vouchsafe."

Considering the costume I saw her son in a few minutes ago, this made me very, very, afraid.

Camelot

We spent the next half hour watching Hope perform a solo costume parade. Wait. Scratch the solo part. After a few minutes, both Sam and Anne joined in, adding to their own personal collections. Sandy's costumes were quite impressive. Some of them were so subtle with the Ren Faire theme that my friends could have gotten away with wearing them on the streets of Malibu. Peasant dresses are always in fashion, after all.

Sandy was racking up quite a few sales before the faire even opened. Hope bought a new dress for each day she expected to be at the faire over the long Labor Day weekend. Even though Hope insisted on paying, Sandy clearly "forgot" to ring up one or two of the outfits when she was tabulating the final purchase. Nobody said anything, though.

"I think you single-handedly paid my rent for the first month in my new store," Sandy said as she ran Hope's credit card through the little electronic machine beside the register. I don't know where the wires were running to on the former golf course, but the House of Sandoval took some fairly modern payment for Renaissance times.

"Store?" Sam asked.

"Caught that, didn't you?" Sandy said. "No wonder Daniel calls me a flibbertigibbit. Can't help myself." She gave a not-so-wistful sigh. "I was going to save it for a big announcement, but I guess it's now or never." Sandy glanced back to her silent husband. I'd forgotten he was even there. "We're giving up on the year-round faire circuit and setting up permanent residence with my sister in San Francisco. She scouted out a primo, permanent location for the House of Sandoval: Fine Purveyors of Modern Clothing with a Classical Flair." She said that last part standing tall and proud.

"Wow," Anne said. "I thought you guys were going to be gypsies for life."

"We wanted Marq to have a senior year in an actual school," Sandy said. "Besides, my big personality, and even bigger mouth can only be contained to an RV for so long."

We all congratulated Sandy on her new life as the women folk turned the conversation back to even more talk about clothing. I had to agree that Sandy's outfits were a great basis for a boutique, especially in boho San Francisco. I was even thinking about breaking down and maybe buying something for myself when trumpets blared, pulling me out of my thoughts.

"The Morning Revels!" Sam cheered. Obviously, she was

speaking in some kind of Ren Faire code that everyone but me and Hope understood.

"Daniel, get the camera!" Sandy ordered as she dashed out of the tent. Her husband took on a panicked quality in the next moment as the clothes around him started flying, scaring us all. Anne and Sam—followed by me and Hope—made our way out from under the canopy to avoid being wounded by the clothing shrapnel.

All the costumed people around us had stopped setting up their booths and carts and were standing along the main thoroughfare. The trumpets sounded again, and all heads turned in our direction for some reason. That's when I saw a pair of men, with those really long trumpets with flags on them that you sometimes see in old cartoons, coming around the corner.

"Daniel! Camera!" Sandy bellowed. There was a muffled response from her husband, but he did not appear.

Anne turned to me. "Bryan?"

"I'm on it," I said, pulling my camera out of one of the many pockets in my Go-Go Gadget Shorts. Then I leaned over to Sam and asked, "What am I shooting?"

"The Morning Revels," she explained without actually explaining anything.

"A little more?" I asked.

"The royal court parades through the fairgrounds every morning before opening," she said.

"Ah," I said, though I didn't get what the excitement was about. I mean, if it happened every morning, I'd have thought everyone would be used to it by now. Then I realized that the royal court probably meant the queen. And the queen meant: Marq.

The trumpets blared again as the court turned the corner. Beginning with a soldier holding up what I assumed to be the banner of Queen Elizabeth, the parade began to pass us by.

Calling it a parade is a bit of an exaggeration. It was less than a dozen people, mostly noble-type men and women and a couple servants. But the big draw had to be the person at the end, Queen Elizabeth.

"Daniel, you're missing your damn son!"

And let me tell you, this was a moment any father would be proud of.

Actually, he was. Daniel made it out beside his lovely wife—sans camera—and the pair of them were positively beaming when they saw their son as the Queen of the Faire. It was kind of nice. I was so busy watching the two of them watch their son that I totally forgot to take his picture.

Until Sam kicked me in the shin.

The sun was so bright that I couldn't see the screen on my digital camera, so I raised the viewfinder to my eye to get the best shot. When I did, I saw Marq, in his painted face, looking right at me again. I ignored his expression while I snapped the shot. I wanted to explain that I wasn't taking the picture for myself—that his dad had lost their camera. But it really wasn't the time or the place to yell that out. Besides, it might have come across as a "he doth protest too much" moment, and I didn't want to give Marq any more ammunition for what he probably already thought.

I got in a couple more shots before the parade was too far down the row to get a clear picture. As the crowd around us dispersed, several of the costumed folk came by to congratulate Sandy and Daniel on their son's accomplishment at making queen. It wasn't a surprise that the faire folk would be so accepting. These were a people who, by their very nature, embraced bravado and flamboyance. Honestly, in my own life, I was surrounded by similar people, which is why I knew when I did formally come out there wasn't going to be anything to fear.

Still, that didn't make me want to rush things. I wasn't ready to be anyone's GBF yet. I was just happy being me.

Once the hubbub died down we all went back into the House of Sandoval talking about how regal Marq looked and how much he carried off the role, with only minimal mention of the fact that the role was that of a girl. With the faire about to open, we all pitched in to get the "store" ready before the first fairegoers arrived. There wasn't all that much to do other than clean up the remnants of the impromptu fashion show. Sandy only made about a half dozen attempts to get me into a pair of her tights.

Wait. That doesn't sound right.

About ten minutes later, trumpets sounded again, alerting us that the gates were now officially opened. Shouts of "Huzzah" rang throughout the general vicinity with Hope and me joining in a few seconds behind. I have to admit that mine was more of a sarcastic "Huzzah," but I'm fairly certain that Sam was the only one who caught on.

Since we were at the end of one of the four rows, it was going to be a few minutes until we had the first customers of the day. I was going to suggest running out for a quick breakfast when I felt someone removing my fedora.

I turned to find Sandy behind me with my fedora in one hand and a poofy purple hat with a narrow brim poised to land on my head. "What are you doing?" I asked.

"If you can't wear a costume, you have to at least accessorize," she said, dropping the hat on my head. "You have the perfect head for an Elizabethan cap." I wasn't sure if that was a compliment. "Here, look in the mirror." She manhandled me toward a mirror so I could check myself out. I have to admit, I did kind of work the hat.

"Fine," I said. "How much?"

She waved me off with a *pffft* sound as she took my fedora to the back for safekeeping.

"You do realize she is going to slowly put you in more of a costume every chance she gets," Sam warned.

"Yeah. We'll see who wins that one."

Neither Sam nor Hope reacted like they thought it would be me. I turned away from them to admire myself for a while in my fancy hat. And because I couldn't think of a snappy comeback.

It didn't take nearly as long as I'd thought for the first guests to arrive at our little canopied corner of the faire to start browsing. Apparently, the House of Sandoval has quite the reputation on the circuit and the hardcore fairegoers sought it out first to get the latest creations. With Anne,

Sandy, Daniel, Hope, Sam, and me trying to help the morning rush, we wound up getting in the way a lot. We were in one of the larger spaces in the faire, but it wasn't exactly a department store.

While I was helping Sam help a young costumed couple outfit their infant in the latest infant fashions from the sixteenth century, my cell phone went off. This earned me sharp looks of reproach from the costumed people in my vicinity. I guess the faire folk had something against modern technology . . . that wasn't associated with credit card transactions, that is. The glances continued while the ringing went on . . . and on. I love my Go-Go Gadget Shorts because they allow me to carry a bunch of stuff without having to resort to a man-purse.

After searching several pockets, I finally extracted the phone from the pocket by my left knee. My whole body tensed when I read the name on the screen.

"It's Drew," I whispered to Sam. I checked to make sure that Hope was busy on the other side of the tent, then stepped behind a rack of velvet robes to answer the phone. She and Drew had dated for several years before breaking up at the Start-of-Summer Beach Party back in June. They eventually parted on good terms before she left for New York, but I wasn't sure if she was ready to deal with him on her first full day back in town.

"Hey," I said answering the phone.

"Hey," he replied, followed by a brief silence on both ends of the call. After being best buds for most of our childhood, Drew and I had a brief period of estrangement—as they say—

before returning to some semblance of a friendship. This largely happened because my current best friend—Sam—was dating his current best friend—Eric. Though we were on much better terms lately, Drew and I clearly had some more work to do on our phone conversational skills. "I'm here," he finally said.

"Here, where?"

"Here, *here*," he replied. "At the entrance."

"You're *here*?"

We *really* needed to work on those phone skills.

"I'm glad we've established that much," Drew said. "Where's Hope? She told me to call you since she doesn't have her cell on her."

"Hope told you to call?"

"Let's not start with the obvious questions again," Drew said.

I didn't respond. It would have been nice for Hope to warn me he was going to call so I didn't have to waste precious empathy points worrying about her. I pushed the velvet robes aside and walked through the rack and across the selling floor. "It's for you," I said handing Hope the cell phone.

"Thanks," she said, not even asking who was on the line. Theirs was a brief conversation that ended with Hope saying, "We'll come get you."

As she handed me back my phone, I had to ask. "You're okay with seeing him?"

"Sure," Hope said. "I told you we talked like every other day over the summer."

"Um . . . no you didn't."

"You told me," Sam chimed in from behind me.

"Oh," Hope said, looking apologetic. People often confuse me with Sam. I understand, considering how I'm, like, a foot taller, have much darker hair . . . and am *male*.

"*You're* okay with him being here, right." Hope addressed this question to me in a tone that was more a threat than an inquiry.

"Totally," I said, in all honesty. With everyone gone for the summer—particularly Hope and Eric—I'd wound up hanging out a lot with Drew. Not like we were entrusting each other with our deepest secrets and having sleepovers like when we were kids. But we grabbed the occasional ice-blended coffees. I was kind of looking forward to seeing him at the faire. Aside from the fact that it meant I wouldn't be the only one sans costume, I figured once Eric got back from vacation with his dad, Drew would forget about me again like he'd done years before.

What? Me bitter?

But the big question was what did this mean for Hope and Drew as a couple? All that talking over the summer? Getting together the first full day she's back in town? Could it be that they were on friendlier than friendship terms?

I wasn't so sure how I felt about that.

"Don't even go there," Hope said, getting all mind-readery. "We're not getting back together. So stop thinking what you're thinking. Drew and I are just friends."

"That's good," Sam said. "Because Eric's coming back—"

"Again," I added.

"—on Monday and I don't want to have to split my time between you and him. It's much easier when we're all one happy little family unit."

"Don't see *that* happening," I mumbled loudly enough for them to hear me but softly enough that they could ignore me, which they both chose to do. I didn't really have the issues with Sam's boyfriend that I used to have. However, he and I did get along much better while he was three thousand miles away and had no contact whatsoever.

"Drew's waiting," Hope reminded us. I couldn't help but notice that she was checking her reflection in a nearby mirror and making a few adjustments to her hair and clothes. She may have spent the summer back in communication with Drew and she may have agreed to be friends, but I figured the first time she saw him in person, she wanted to remind him of what he was no longer getting.

Sam, too, was checking herself out and readjusting before she left. That bodice did not look all that comfortable. And it was still making me considerably uncomfortable as well. I tore my eyes away from her and grabbed a quick ego check of myself in the mirror. I toyed with the idea of stealing my fedora back, but the Elizabethan cap that Sandy had slammed on my head did give me a rakish quality that I kind of liked. I tipped it slightly to the side to give it more of a devil-may-care vibe.

After asking permission to ditch our serving duties, we set out for the entrance. At first it was fairly sparse with people since we were at the back end of the faire. It quickly got more crowded the more we swam upstream. Many of the people flooding past us were also dressed in faire regalia while the others were stopping to take pictures. All along the way, people were shouting out "Good morrow!" and other friendly greetings. And those people with the HUG ME signs were getting a fair amount of action too.

"This is like the second happiest freakin' place on Earth," Hope said.

"Annoying, isn't it?" I agreed.

"Not nearly as annoying as the two of you," Sam said as we hit the front part of the faire. It was slow moving against the sea of people coming in from the entrance. I never realized that there would be such a turnout. And it was only the first hour of the first day. There was still an entire long weekend of fair-going to go.

Hope hopped up on a bench to be the lookout. "We are never going to find—"

"There he is," I said, picking out Drew's red T-shirt among a gaggle of fairegoers dressed in wintertime caroling outfits. They were all *way* too bundled up in their woolens for the first weekend of September, and would likely come to regret their choice of apparel somewhere around midday.

Drew seemed hopelessly out of place in their midst in his red T, brown shorts, and baseball cap. Normally, I could list exactly where he purchased the components of his outfit as the names of the stores would be emblazoned across his chest or his butt in some immodest display of advertising. But there was nary a label to be seen when we finally managed to fight

Paul Ruditis

our way through the crowd and saw him up close and personal. Even the ball cap was logo-free.

"How did I let you talk me into coming here?" Drew asked
as he and Hope embraced in a surprisingly comfortable looking hug. Notably, there was no kiss . . . unlike Marq, earlier.

"Tell me about it," I said.

"What?" Drew said as he switched hugging partners to
Sam. "I thought this would be your kind of thing."

"You thought wrong," I said.

"Your mouth says one thing, but your hat says another," he
replied. "You look like a tall, skinny, mushroom."

I'd forgotten I was wearing the Elizabethan cap. What had
seemed rakish only moments ago now made me feel foolish. I
think I blushed the same color of red that was in Drew's shirt
while I considered losing the hat altogether. Then a family in
chocolate brown monk's robes passed us and I didn't feel
nearly as out of place.

I rolled my eyes in their direction and Drew gave a shrug
like he got the hat thing. We exchanged the "straight-guy
hug," patting each other on the back enthusiastically to keep
us from an actual embrace. I don't know at what point in our
lives our childhood hugs became fraught with such danger
that we needed to seem all the more manly whenever we
greeted each other this way.

Actually, maybe I do.

"Where do we start?" Drew asked, taking in the surroundings.

"I want you to meet Marq," Sam said. "He should be set up
by the entrance."

It wasn't hard for us to find him. The queen's stage was off to the left under a canopy draped with ribbons and flowers. Marq was sitting on a high-backed antique chair with several attendants. They were greeting a line of fairegoers as they came in, receiving them as if they were royal guests. When he saw us looking in his direction, he waved in a frantic, rather un-queenlike manner that drew expressions of reproach from the attendants around him.

"Maybe we should save that for later," I suggested, worrying that if we did go up to him, he'd overflow with the same enthusiasm he'd had meeting Hope and me earlier, and get into trouble for not behaving in a manner befitting a queen. That, and freak out Drew as well. Drew wasn't a Drama Geek like the rest of us. He was handling the whole Ren Faire thing rather well for a soccer player, but I suspected that he'd have his limit. Marq could very well be that limit.

"Yeah," Hope agreed. "He's too busy playing the Virgin Queen anyway."

There was something about what she said that started nagging at the back of my mind.

"You remember when Grandpa Willie brought us here to teach us how to play golf?" Drew asked me, pulling me out of my thoughts.

"And we started making castles in the sand traps," I recalled. This earned us odd looks from Sam and Hope. "What? We were six."

"Bet he'd love to see a Renaissance Faire taking over the course," Drew added.

"He'd still play through," I said, trying to catch that fleeting thought that had recently escaped me. "But at least our sand castles would be more fitting in the surroundings."

"Anybody up for some breakfast?" Sam asked. "We can get some kick-butt smoothies at this place called The Unicorn Horn."

And there it was; the rogue thought. No. Make that fear.

My eyes were drawn back to the unnerving display of Sam's rather buxom chest. I finally figured out what it was about her outfit that was bothering me so much.

I wasn't freaked out by what was right there in front of me.

I was freaked out by what *wasn't*.

I Never Sang for My Father

Sam's necklace was gone.

Her silver unicorn necklace.

Sam had been wearing her unicorn necklace every single day since we'd first met. Every single day since long *before* we'd met. She once made the mistake of telling—I *mean*, she once confided in—me that she was only going to take it off after her first time. And if you wonder what "first time" I'm referring to, let me remind you that it was the "Virgin Queen" comment that tipped me off to this stunning new development. See, mythologically speaking, unicorns are all about the virgins. According to legend, they only appear to girls with their virtue intact. And, as you can tell by the whole Renaissance Faire thing, Sam takes her mythology of the time period very seriously.

After Sam had told me about the necklace, I'd developed the nervous habit of constantly checking to make sure she was still wearing it. I became particularly obsessive about it when she started dating Eric. Until one day when she caught me doing it and yelled at me about it. I'd like to say that I stopped looking altogether, but I'd been stealing peeks every now and again.

I probably would have noticed sooner, but with Eric gone for the past six weeks visiting his mom, there didn't seem to be any reason to keep up on that kind of thing. It wasn't like Sam was a wanton woman or anything.

Eric had only been home for one day last week before going back off on vacation with his dad, so I hadn't really given the necklace any thought. I guess this told me how they reconnected before he went off again. Just to be clear, Sam sleeping with Eric wasn't that big of a surprise. Okay, they've only been together about four months and he's been gone for a long chunk of that, but he's her first real boyfriend. I know how much she likes him. Much as I like to bust on him, Eric's actually a pretty decent guy. Especially toward Sam. Which makes him even more annoyingly perfect as far as I'm concerned. And, okay, I guess he's kind of hot. There could be worse guys to lose it to.

Then again, it was possible that maybe the clasp had just broken. Or maybe she was having it cleaned. It could have been gone for a totally innocuous reason. Something as earth-shattering as Sam's first time would be the kind of thing she would usually run to tell me about.

At least, that's what I thought.

Hope interrupted my musings by yelling, "Incoming!" as a flurry of white and gold came running at us. Her survival reflexes took over, pulling Drew out of danger as a boy in a big dress nearly collided with her ex-boyfriend.

"Ohmigod!" Marq squealed at us, his mouth going a hundred miles an hour. "That laced mutton, Jocelyn, got done her audition and raced back here just so she could kick me out of the queen's chair in front of the entire court." He yelled in the queen's general direction, "Fie! You gorbellied doxy!" Then, back to us. "Like I'd want to spend any more time sitting where her big, smelly butt sat, thank you very much. Now, I've got to get out of my dress because we can't have two queens running around the faire."

"Perish the thought," I managed to slip in.

"Meet us at the Court of Savory Treats," Sam called to him as he dashed off. "Oh, and Marq, this is our friend Drew."

Running backward—in a dress no less—he squealed again. "You know the *cutest* boys!" And he was gone into the crowd.

"What? Was that?" Drew asked.

"Marq," Sam, Hope, and I said as if it explained everything. And it kind of did.

"I'm *starving*," I whined. I think this was the longest I'd been up without having anything to eat in my life. But the empty space in my stomach could not entirely overshadow the empty space at the bottom of Sam's neck. This was so not the time or the place for the conversation, but maybe once I got some food in me I'd figure out a way to bring it up without her bringing down a tankard of whoop-ass on me.

"This way," Sam directed as we pushed our way through the crowd.

Peddlers all around us were calling out, trying to draw the tourists in to buy their wares. "Chain mail! Spit polished chain mail!" a burly man with a scraggy beard shouted out from a fenced-off area filled with armor of various shapes and sizes.

"Snake oil!" a shrill woman's voice rang out from an apothecary tent. "Pox cures. Herbal remedies for the ills that vex thee."

"Marry! Come ye lads and lasses, bear witness to sights that will blow thine minds," said a man standing beside a mysterious small rectangular building the size and shape of an outhouse. I wasn't the only person letting that one go unexplored.

Stained glass artwork, jewelry, and various handmade items were being exchanged for modern money all around us. The cynic in me suspected that this was more what the faire was about than any merriment celebrating life in a different era, but I wasn't going to say that aloud. Especially since I was hoping to use my connection to Sam to maybe get some discounts with a few of these sellers. I was eyeing a stellar tapestry of a dragon in flight that would look great on my bedroom wall. When the shop owner shouted out a "Good morrow, Samantha!" in our direction, I made a mental note to bring her back there to say a more proper hello after we ate.

If my internal GPS was right, we were getting closer to the faire's food court, which is why it was such a surprise when Sam stopped in front of a large, black tent.

Can't say that there were many people doing the same.

Ominous is a word I don't use all that often. Or, if I do, I'm usually exaggerating for humorous effect. This time? Not so much. This tent was ominous. And I wasn't the only one who noticed. People were subtly moving away from the tent as they passed in either a conscious or unconscious desire to get away.

First of all, it was the only full tent I'd seen since I'd arrived at the faire. Most tents were merely canopies, like the House of Sandoval. They were open and welcoming, and didn't even have walls, just posts to hold up the roof. This one did. Four black walls with hand-sewn patches from top to bottom in what must have been an ongoing battle to keep the weathered old tent alive. Small tears peeked out all along the front of the tent. The bottoms of the walls that I could see were frayed, obviously from years in service.

One shadowy entrance stood before us with a pair of torches on wooden posts on either side. A fire hazard for sure, but an effective way of setting the mood. And the mood it set was dark and evil. No peddler stood outside trying to draw people in to spend their money. In fact, there was no indication at all what they would find once they crossed the threshold.

If a tent could be haunted, this would be that tent.

"What is this place?" I asked.

"Jeremy's tent," Sam said in my direction. "You're going to *love* this."

I didn't know who this Jeremy person was, but I had to admit I liked him already. His tent wasn't all about making a sale, like the other peddlers around us. At least, it didn't seem that way from the outside. If anything, it seemed the most Renaissance-like of anything I'd seen since we got there. I don't know what tents really looked like back then, but I wouldn't have been surprised if this one had been picked up out of that era and dropped right in the middle of the golf course.

"Come on," Sam said, rushing into the tent.

Hope, Drew, and I followed slowly, pausing at the threshold. The sign above the entryway gave us no indication of what to expect. All it did was warn. ABANDON ALL HOPE, YE WHO ENTER HERE.

Drew and I turned to our friend standing between us and said, "Good-bye, Hope," abandoning her to go inside.

"Very funny," she said, smacking us both in the backs of our heads as she pushed past us.

The tent interior was no more welcoming than the exterior had been, but it was way wicked cool. The few electric lights inside cast a dim glow that helped with the mood. Whoever this Jeremy was, he liked some dark and disturbing things.

Gargoyle statues, realistic skulls, and crystal balls filled the shelves around us. A pile of wooden stakes sat on a pedestal by the door with a sign that read IN CASE OF VAMPIRE ATTACK. Darkly mysterious paintings of vicious creatures hung from posts running along the tent flaps. I was already calculating the money in my wallet—which I knew to be in my left, back pocket—as I eyed a metal pentagram that would look great over my bed. (*Aside:* Before you go thinking I'm all satanic, allow me to point out that a pentagram is often considered a symbol representing the elements of Earth, Air, Water, and Fire, along with Spirit. It's only when you turn it upside down that you're calling on Beelzebub . . . or death-metal fans.)

Not surprisingly, it wasn't very crowded inside the Tent of Darkness (as I had recently decided to call it). In fact, it was fairly empty. Besides us, there were only a middle-aged couple of vampire wannabes, a tall man with long white hair streaked with blue, and his petite wife in black leggings and a top that appeared to have come from a set of red silk pajamas. When the man smiled at me, revealing pointed teeth, I worried that maybe he took this role-playing thing a little too far and I hurried to the other side of the tent. You know, near the wooden stakes.

Sam seemed to be the only one who noticed. "Nice move, Braveheart."

I was just about to cut her down with a fangworthy biting retort when a deep, masculine voice yelled out, "Samwise Gamgee!!"

With a bounding step, a man of about my parents' age fell upon us, scattering me and Hope as he wrapped Sam up in his rather impressively bulging biceps. He effortlessly lifted her off the ground and twirled her around in the kind of hug one simply does not see in the Los Angeles area. I must say, I don't often go in for older men, but he was quite the strapping fellow.

"Jeremiah!" Sam squealed in glee while gasping for breath. I guess it was a really tight hug, especially when she took in a deep breath the moment he put her back down on the ground.

"Thou are wondrous fair, milady," he said, giving Sam the once over, but not in a squicky way. It was almost fatherly. Maybe he was an uncle or something. Once he was satisfied with how Sam was growing up, he performed a quick visual search of the store. "But where art thou mother?"

"Assisting at the House of Sandoval," Sam said, then quickly added, "But I know she is hoping to see you."

"God's teeth, that woman is bemadding," he said. "I must away."

"Wait!" Sam said as he started for the exit. "I'd first present my chatmates, Hope, Bryan, and Drew. Guys, this is Jeremy, an old friend of my parents."

"Hail and well-met," Jeremy said as he wrapped Hope up in one of his welcoming hugs. As he let her go, I prepared myself for an embrace and was disappointed when he only put out his hand for me to shake.

What a gyp!

As his hand engulfed Drew's, I realized that Sam had referred to her parents in the plural sense, something she rarely does. Sam's dad disappeared way back when she was five and hasn't been seen since. We didn't talk about him much. Ever.

"Perchance, this lovely songbird will enchant us with a tune at a later time? Wouldst thou?" Jeremy asked Sam once the introductions were complete. Somehow, I didn't think Jeremy was half as annoying with the "thees" and the "thous" as I had found other people to be since coming to the faire.

"Mayhap," Sam replied. Yeah, like she'd ever turn down a chance to sing for an audience.

"Until then," he said, making another move for the exit. "I shall see you anon! Harrison, watch the store!" That last part was directed to a guy standing behind the back counter.

And with that, Jeremy was gone.

"He sure is in a rush to see Anne," I said.

"They go way back," Sam said. "Jeremy introduced my parents to the whole Renaissance Faire world. And to each other."

I suspected Jeremy's desire to see Anne had something more than friendship to it, but I didn't say anything. I was too busy exchanging knowing glances with Hope. It was extremely rare that Sam let us into this part of her life and her MIA D-A-D. I guess Drew picked up on what was happening, because he suddenly found great interest in the weapons collection hanging on a nearby rack.

"You okay?" I asked her softly.

"Yeah," Sam said with a half shrug. "My dad's kind of tied to this place, so I'm used to it. Here. Check this out."

We started toward the back of the store when a loud crash brought our attention to Drew. He was knee deep in swords as the entire rack he had been looking at collapsed around him. Even in the shadowy tent, I could see his face was blood red with embarrassment.

"Oh, crap," he said, scrambling to fix the swords. "I'm so sorry."

"That's okay," the guy Jeremy left in charge said. "That rack is defective. We need to put it in back before it really hurts someone."

"Sorry," Drew said again as he picked up—then dropped—one of the larger swords.

"I'd better help before he kills himself," Hope said. She gently pushed us to continue where Sam had been leading. All in all, the unintentional distraction worked out fairly well considering all the attention was now focused on the sword display while Sam led me to the back wall.

"Here it is," she said, pointing to a sepia-toned photograph hanging beside the counter.

Two rows of costumed adults posed in front of what appeared to be a much newer version of the tent we were standing in. They looked almost like one of those photos in the Harry Potter movies and I was kind of surprised that the people weren't moving and waving to us. But this was just a simple, nonmagical photo with mortal people. The sepia tone was just added to give it a more old-fashioned look.

The back row of people were standing up, posed with smiles on their faces, while the front row was hunched down on their knees. Two little kids—a girl and a boy, also dressed like a little maid and master—played at the adults' feet, unaware of the camera. I swore I saw a little glint of light flashing off the girl's neck, right where a silver unicorn might be.

"Is that you?" I asked. "You and . . . Marq?"

She mumbled something and nodded, causing me to notice

exactly how far away she seemed to be, standing there right next to me. Clearly, she hadn't brought me over just to look at baby pictures.

"Your dad?" I asked, scanning the picture. Sam never had any photos of him out at home. I'd never asked to see any either. "Which one?" I asked, examining the rows of people.

"Standing next to my mom," she said with no small amount of annoyance in her tone.

Yeah, I should have figured that one out.

A nearly dozen years younger version of Anne was standing dead center in the back row with a guy that had to have been Jeremy on her left and a man wearing rectangular glasses on her right. He wasn't all that big in the picture, but I could see a bit of a resemblance between Sam and him, particularly in the way he was posing. I'd seen Sam strike that same stance in many of the pictures I'd taken of her over the past few years.

"You don't think . . ." I wasn't sure how to ask this question. "Is there a chance he could show up here?"

Sam's calculated lack of reaction was more unnerving than the empty spot at the base of her neck. "Hasn't turned up in the last decade," Sam said. "Doubt it would happen now. I don't think he'd get past the front gate anyway. Too many people here are still mad at him for how he disappeared from Mom and me. They'd probably have him lashed to the rack before he got more than a few steps inside."

Now I had another question I didn't know how to ask. See, Sam and me, we didn't talk much about her missing dad. It always felt like I was prying. Sure, we'd joke around from time to time about missing fathers since my dad was always off on international travel for his mysterious job. But Dad's travels were a far more recent development in our lives. Not to mention that he always came back home. Or called. Or e-mailed. Or found a million ways to make contact, which Sam's father couldn't manage in the years since he'd left.

Sam was never one with the free flow of information on the subject of her missing father. For the first time in our friendship I kind of felt like she was eager to talk about it, so I plunged ahead. "Do you want him to show up?"

"I gave up on wanting that years ago," she said.

"But if he did," I said, "what would you do?"

Sam thought about it for a moment. I can't imagine it was the first time she'd considered that same question. Her response probably changed hundreds of times through the years, depending on the place she was at in her life. "I'd probably tell him to go to hell," she said in a rather final sounding way. I still had a bunch of questions swirling around in my mind, but her body language and tight face told me that the door that she had finally opened a crack had just been slammed shut.

Besides, we were distracted when our best friend suddenly decided to go insane.

Measure for Measure

"Oooo, ooo, oooo," Hope burst out in what sounded very much like monkey talk. I'm guessing she must have been watching us stand in silence for a while since she wouldn't have interrupted otherwise. Although, there was no telling whether or not she'd gone and lost her damn mind, what with the "Oooo, ooo, oooos."

She was holding an old quill pen and had that expression on her face that she generally had when inspiration struck. See, Hope's the writer in our group. Usually poems. Often about her dead dog. But she didn't generally get this excited over an entry in her *Book of the Dead Puppy Poetry, Volume Six*. This had to be serious inspiration. Possibly a poem of epic proportions. Even the wannabe vamps were looking at us as if we were all crazy, which is saying something. You know . . . considering.

"How can this place have pens, but nothing to write on?"

she asked, waving the feathered pen in front of my eyes. She held a hand out to me. "Give me your phone."

"What?"

"Phone. Now." She didn't bother waiting, grabbing at the many pockets in my Go-Go Gadget Shorts. Including the ones in less than accessible places.

"Hey!" I shouted, slapping her hands away. "I can get it myself." I reached into the phone pocket and retrieved what she had been searching for. "Who are you calling?" I asked as I handed my cell phone to her. "All of your friends are here."

"Nice," Drew said as he joined us.

"All *my* friends are here too," I replied. "If it's an insult for her, it's an insult for me." As soon as she had the phone, she took off to the other side of the tent so that we could not listen in, which was smart, because Sam and I are the type who would totally eavesdrop.

"What about Suze?" Drew asked, making way more out of my lame attempt at a joke than was necessary. "I thought you guys were . . . friends?"

"We are," I said, trying to sound noncommittal. The "friend" part of Drew's question *was* up in the air. Suze had been my friend for many years, and more recently, my date for the junior prom. Before she'd left for a summer internship in New York, I'd had the distinct impression that she wanted to become something more than friends. Apparently, I wasn't the only one who had noticed.

Hope saved us from any further unpleasant discussion by

coming back to us and handing me my flip phone, which was still open. "It's for you," she said.

"I know," I said. "It's my phone."

"I mean Suze's on the line," Hope said. "She called in while I was leaving myself a message. I switched over when I saw her name on the caller ID."

"Oh." It was like Suze knew we'd been talking about her. I worried that the magical items in the room weren't simply dust collectors like I thought. Maybe they did have real paranormal powers. Like contacting the person you wanted to speak to the least upon the mention of her name.

I'd been—well, there's no better way to say this—*avoiding* Suze for the past couple weeks. Since she left for New York back at the end of June, barely a day had gone by without a call or a text from her. I can't imagine she was all that bored in one of the most exciting cities in the world. Our more recent calls had been taking a more decidedly romantic turn since the start of August. Or, I should say, her side of our calls had been that way, with the "I really miss you" and the "can't wait to see you again." Since I didn't want to lead her on, I'd been kind of avoiding her. No. That sounds harsh. Let's say that I have been making tactical decisions not to answer my phone on the occasions that it rang.

Unless one of my friends answers it for me and shoves it in my hand.

Not that I hadn't considered coming out to Suze and saving us both from the embarrassment. But every time I thought it through, it just seemed so presumptuous. I mean, maybe I'd been making up all of her interest in me in my mind. Maybe she only wanted to be friends. How embarrassing would it be to just blurt out that I was gay and have her all, "So, why are you telling me?"

"Hey, Suze," I said, moving over to the entryway so I could have some privacy in case the call got awkward.

"Bryan!" she said. "Don't you ever answer your phone anymore?"

"I've been working a lot at my mom's new store," I said, which was true. "I get horrible reception there." Which was false.

"Hope told me you guys are at some Renaissance Faire?" Suze asked.

"Yes. Yes we are."

"I'm picturing you, right now, in a dark green lord's shirt with black laces up the front, a pair of brown baggy pantaloons that tie at the ankles, and a pair of black tights peeking out from your Peter Pan slippers," she said. Suze was a soon-to-be famous fashion designer, after all.

"Not quite," I said. "I'm in shorts and a button-down shirt. Sam and Hope have gone the costume route, though."

"Pity," Suze said. "Because you look really cute in the outfit I'm imagining. Maybe we can get you in one when I get back."

"More forceful women than you have tried," I said, thinking back to Marq's mom with a shudder. "I *am* wearing a purple Elizabethan cap. That's about as far as I'm willing to go."

"We'll see about that," she said. "Pick me up from the airport Sunday so I can start working on you."

"Well . . . ," I said, noncommittally.

"Please," she added. "Mom is going with Dad to one of his work retreats this weekend. She usually hates those things, but her not being home when I get in is her passive-aggressive way of reminding me she didn't want me coming to New York in the first place." Suze's mom always wanted her in front of the camera, not behind a sketchbook.

Committing to a ride from the airport seemed like a deeply personal favor—boyfriend level, even. Not that the airport was far or anything. It was just one of those pictures you have in your mind. Like waiting by the luggage carousel with a bouquet of flowers for your true love to return.

Oddly, my imaginings never had Suze in the picture. Or any girl, for that matter.

Still, I couldn't leave her stranded. Add in the fringe benefit that it would get me out of spending all day Sunday at the faire and clearly I was going to give her the ride. I just needed to figure out how to agree to it without giving her the wrong idea.

Too bad I didn't have a chance.

At that exact moment, a pair of hands grabbed the back of my shirt, pulling me out of the dark tent and into the blindingly bright sunlight. "Hey!" I shouted, throwing a squinting glance over my shoulder. Sam's GBF, Marq, was dragging me off for some reason. For a thin wisp of a guy, he sure had a mighty grip.

"What's wrong?" Suze asked. Her voice was filled with genuine concern.

"Nothing," I said, lightly. "I'm being kidnapped." Though it was annoying, it did present me with an opportunity. "I gotta go," I added. "Send me your flight info. I'll be there."

"Thanks," she said with uncertainty.

"Later," I said as I hung up my phone. This was certainly a weird predicament. I had a girl that I thought wanted to be my girlfriend on the phone, while a boy who I didn't want to *know* what he wanted with me was dragging me off to who knew where.

It's an odd life that I lead.

I turned my head in Marq's direction, which was awkward since I was walking—or stumbling—backward at the time. At least he was dressed in boy's clothes now, in an outfit that was shockingly close to the one Suze had pictured me wearing. "Out of curiosity . . . where do you think you're taking me?"

"You'll see," he said.

I considered breaking free of his stranglehold, when I saw Sam following with Drew and Hope in tow. Sam was smiling, which went a long way to making me feel better about this whole thing. After the moment we had talking about her father, it was nice to see her getting some life back in her. So I decided to go along with Marq's crazy game for her benefit.

I know. Noble, aren't I?

"Can you at least let me turn around?" I asked. "I'm going to break my neck."

"Aye," he said, twisting the back of my T-shirt so that I could spin along with it. He kept his hand clamped down on me while he continued to drag me through the crowd. My kewl new Elizabethan cap fell off in the process, but

Sam retrieved it and she picked up the pace along with us.

"Sam. Care to tell me what he's doing?"

"Marq, what are you doing?" she asked.

Thanks. I could have done that. Oh wait. I did.

"Your darling little friend here was using a cell phone," he replied.

"Darling?" Drew laughed.

"You're Drew, right?" Marq asked, checking Drew up and down without breaking stride. "Hail and well-met!" Since I was so close, I heard Marq add, softly, *"Really* well-met."

Once Marq was done checking Drew out, he returned his attention to me. For a brief moment, I'd kind of hoped that Drew's presence would shift Marq's attention permanently off me, but no such luck. I'm sure if I'd really had the chance to think that one over, Marq making goo-goo eyes at Drew would have been the last thing I'd have wanted, but the hunger from skipping breakfast was starting to affect my mind.

And Marq had just dragged me past the food court!

"Wherever we're going, can we stop and eat first?" I asked.

"Nay, gentle friend," he replied. "Justice waits for no man. Or morsel."

I rolled my eyes as he gave me a tug forward. "What justice? What's this about me being on my cell phone? We've passed at least a dozen people on their cell phones."

"Patrons of the faire," he explained. "Costumed revelers are not permitted to use modern technology in the presence of faire guests," he explained.

"Costumed?" I asked. I was too stuck on that to even

question the whole "revelers" thing. I don't know that I've ever *reveled*. "I was wearing a cap. A cap that your mother forced me to wear when she took my fedora! A cap that I don't even have on my head anymore." That's when Sam got all helpful and put the hat back on me. "Thanks," I growled.

"Attacking my mother is not going to get you out of trouble," Marq said as he started skipping. *Skipping!*

It was all I could do to stay on my feet as he pulled me along. I steadfastly refused to skip. Unfortunately, that meant that I had to jog to keep up.

"Get thee to the pillory!" he sang.

"You're taking me to the drugstore?"

"That's an apothecary," Sam said.

"Oh." She was being quite the help. Yet, she still didn't answer my question. That only came when we rounded the bend past the wedding pavilion and I saw a small platform with a pair of wooden T-bars with three holes in each. A balding man was already locked in one with his head and hands trapped around him. His family was off to the side taking pictures. "You're putting me in the stocks?" I asked.

"Pillory," the short, stout girl manning the platform corrected. She was dressed in black executioner's robes, with a hood hanging from the back of her neck. I didn't want to know what punishment would warrant her slipping the hood on, but there was a scary looking guillotine beside the platform. "The stocks be for thy legs. A common mistake." The girl, who looked about our age turned to Marq. "What be the lad's crime?"

"Improper use of anachronistic technology," Marq said, holding out my cell phone as Exhibit A.

"But he's not in costume," the girl noted, slipping out of character. Finally! Someone who saw the logic.

Marq held me away from him as he leaned into the girl and whispered through clenched teeth, "Just go with it, Drea." The girl shrugged, took me by the arm and pulled me up on the platform.

"Be sure to get the guillotine in the picture," the man already up there said with glee as his wife lined up a shot of him and his kids.

"Into the pillory with you, lad," Marq said, giving me a shove from behind.

I shot him a death glare over my shoulder. My death glare was nothing compared to Hope's, but it was the only weapon I had in my arsenal at the moment. This was *so* not the way for him to make a first impression on Sam's BF.

Marq returned my glare with a huge smile. Maybe I was misreading the grin, but he seemed to be saying, "Play along, or else."

Worrying about the implied, "or else," I moved around to the back of the pillory and stuck my head and arms in the U-shaped impressions in the wood. The girl then slammed the brace down on me, locking me in. As Rudolph said when his dad stuck that plastic nose on him to cover his shiny, red one, "It's not vewy comfable."

First off, you're stuck in a hunched position that, quite frankly, is not natural. Oh, and your butt is sticking out to everyone peeking in from the next row over. So, that's always nice. The wrist holes on the thing were loose enough that I could slip my hands through in an emergency escape attempt, but my fat head wasn't moving anywhere.

And don't even get me started on the splinters.

"How long do I have to stay in this thing?" I asked.

"Term of punishment for the use of anachronistic technology is thirty minutes," the girl intoned ominously.

"A half hour!" I shouted.

"Don't worry," the guy in the other pillory chuckled. "After the first ten minutes, the time flies by. But that could have something to do with the numbness in my lower extremities."

Easy for him to say. His kids were sitting on the platform posing with him happily. I only had my friends and a small crowd gawking at me. "What did you do to get in here?" I asked.

"Wouldn't let the kids go on the pony rides," he explained. "Apparently, there's a rule about the inhibition of fun at the faire." He said this with a smile, so I'm figuring that it wasn't too serious a crime for him to play along.

"Anybody got any tomatoes we can throw?" Drew asked.

"Don't even think about it," I warned. "And somebody turn my cap around so the back of my neck doesn't burn." Sam hopped up onstage and did as I asked. "You know," I said, "technically, Hope was the one using my phone. And she's in full costume."

"Which one be Hope?" the executioner asked.

Hope raised her hand, throwing me a death glare and an "I dare you" look at the executioner.

"Yeah," the girl said. "The executioner ain't messing with her."

Looking at Hope, I saw a certain logic in the executioner's words. Yet, I had every intention of finding a way to get back at Hope since this was All. Her. Fault.

"I'm guessing this is Drea," Sam said, referring to the afore-mentioned friend that Marq had said earlier had "dungeon duty." The bright sunny day wasn't all that "dungeon" like, but I wasn't about to nitpick. Who knew what kind of prison they could send me to for complaining?

Marq introduced us all to Drea, whom he explained was a more recent member of the faire family. She'd only been touring with them since the summer began. Drea seemed pleasant enough for an executioner. Friendly, even, consid-ering it was her job to punish dangerous criminals who had to take phone calls.

"Thy time is served," Drea announced, releasing the man beside me.

"Actually, I think he's got at least another five minutes," his wife gleefully corrected from behind her camera.

Drea picked up her axe and glared, "You dare question the will of the executioner!" This brought out squeals of fright-ened laughter from the kiddies as their father exited the stage. The family was smiling as they left, so I'm pretty sure they got the most of their faire experience.

"Don't worry, Bryan," Hope said. "This executioner seems to like letting people off easy. I would have locked the wife up for five minutes just because she contradicted me."

Paul Ruditis

"Actually, she was right. He had ten minutes left on his sentence," Drea said. "But the kids were annoying me. They kept trying to play with the guillotine when I wasn't looking."

"Why isn't the blade up?" Sam asked, looking over the death device in a way that made me nervous. It was a tall rectangular wooden structure with a metal blade in the down position, where a person's head would normally go before the beheading. I could only imagine that the blade was a fake. I doubted that the faire was insured for accidental dismemberment.

"It's jammed," Drea explained as the focus went off me for the moment. "I can't raise it by myself. I was going to see if I could get some of the bigger guys to help out later."

"Bigger guys!" Hope said. "I'm sure we could do it ourselves. Here, let me try."

Hope walked over to the rope that lifted the blade. She gave it a good tug and I saw the machine shake, but the blade didn't move. "Drew, come help me with this."

"Sorry," Drea said. "But only people in costume are allowed to touch the equipment.

"Aw, shucks," Drew said. "Looks like I'm off the manual labor today."

Hope glared at him in a playful way. In the past, I would have expected a fight to grow out of this. Maybe they do work better as friends than a couple.

"But we could give it a try," Drea said, moving in behind Hope and grabbing onto the rope.

"Are you planning on helping?" Hope asked Sam.

"Come on, Sammy," Marq said. "Let's show 'em what us girls can do." I guess Marq forgot he was no longer in a dress. Or that, you know, he's actually a *boy*.

The four of them took the rope and gave it a mighty yank, forcing the blade to budge . . . about one centimeter.

Drew hopped up on the platform beside me to get a better view. He also leaned an elbow on the back of my neck, which was quite annoying. "Looks like they showed us guys," he said.

"Maybe we should help by shouting encouragements," I suggested.

"A noble suggestion, old chap," he said, getting off my neck and stepping to the side of the platform. "Heave!"

"Ho," I added.

"Heave," he repeated.

"Ho," I said again.

Drew turned to me. "Are you calling my ex-girlfriend a 'ho'?"

"Oh, I'm sorry," I said. "I guess you'd prefer to do that."

"Thank you," Drew said.

"Anytime," I nodded and yelled, "Heave!"

And Drew added, "Ho!"

Hope stopped her tugging and turned to Sam. "I can't take them as chums."

Marq leaned in and said, "Start hoisting, wench."

Hope hauled off and smacked him, knocking him on his ass. Not that it was that much of an accomplishment. The guy was so lanky he made me look like Star Jones pre–medical intervention.

Speaking of which . . .

"Can someone get me something to eat?" I asked. "A pickle or something! I've got money in the front right pocket of the Go-Go Gadget Shorts."

"I'll get it!" Marq offered, knocking Drew out of the way as he ran onto the platform.

"Never mind!" I quickly said before he could get too grabby.

I'd rather starve.

Damn Yankees!

The girls—and Marq—gave up on the malfunctioning guillotine after a few minutes of pointless exertion. They did manage to get the blade to rise a few inches, but that baby was busted. Hope was the first to pull up some ground for a seat, but the rest eventually joined her to chat while I baked in the heat.

Even with the ocean breeze, it was starting to get uncomfortable on the little wooden platform. The real problem wasn't so much the heat as the stupidity. I was feeling rather lame standing, hunched over, locked in the stocks—I'm sorry, pillory—while it seemed like half the populace of the Los Angeles area passed us by. The giggling children were annoying. The pointing adults were embarrassing. But it was the costumed faire folk that truly grated on my last nerve with their catcalls and shouts of "Scurvy knave!" and "Milksop!"

All the while my friends sat around gossiping with Marq

and Drea about living the faire life. I didn't know what Marq thought he was pulling by having me locked up, but it wasn't endearing me to him any. Every time I considered saying something, I caught him looking at me with a smirk that made me afraid of what he could say in return.

Don't get me wrong. I wasn't really afraid of him outing me. Actually, that would probably make things easier. The last thing I wanted was to make my coming out into a big deal. It's not like I have any control over it. I may be a Drama Geek, but I've never loved being the center of attention. I prefer people to talk about me for the interesting things that I do, not because I made some big Coming Out Proclamation.

Why can't it just be assumed and we can all move on?

And why can't they let me out of the damn pillory!

Only one weekend left in my summer vacation and I was spending it grappling with my identity while suffering public humiliation at a Renaissance Faire. It would be at this point that some people might say, "Things couldn't get any worse." Ah, but I know better than to tempt fate by saying that aloud. Too bad fate is a cruel mistress who likes to play by her own rules where thoughts are as good as words.

"I believe I recognize some familiar faces in period clothing."

And I believe I recognized that voice.

"Headmaster Collins!" Sam said mirroring the shock that I felt. "Mrs. Collins! What are you doing here?"

"Samantha," the headmaster said, and I could see Sam cringe over the use of her full, given name. I guess it's okay from people in costume to use, but anyone in modern dress pronounces it wrong or something. I don't know. "Your mother has said such fascinating things about this fine endeavor of historical recreation, that I and my wife felt that we must check it out."

Why do I always get a headache whenever Headmaster Collins speaks?

"And is that young Mr. Stark in the stocks?" the headmaster asked. Sure. Nobody corrected *him* to say that it was a pillory.

"Hi," I said, lifting my head and peeking out from under my puffy cap. "How's Canoodle?" I'd helped watch the headmaster's dog while he and his wife were on vacation earlier in the summer. She and I bonded during a particularly harsh time in my life.

"She's doing wonderfully," Mrs. Collins enthused. "But I can tell she misses that new friend she made while staying with you. We must arrange a playdate for her and that Labrador of yours, Maleficent." I nodded in noncommittal agreement. The black Lab belonged to my mom's best friend, so I didn't feel it was my place to go making plans . . . or playdates, even. Unless I needed some kind of extracredit during the school year, that is. Then it wouldn't hurt to have the headmaster's wife on my side.

"And what infraction did you commit to find yourself locked in the stocks?" Headmaster Collins asked, calling it by the wrong name again.

"Listening to my friends when they said it would be fun to come to this thing," I replied.

Adding injury to insult, Sam kicked me in the shin again. She did it subtly, so the headmaster didn't notice. But she did it all the same. Not wanting to get into a fight in front of the headmaster, I simply growled at her.

What? We had been talking about dogs, after all.

"This is certainly a spectacle," Headmaster Collins said, taking in his surroundings. "To think that grown adults play dress-up in this manner. Samantha, I am so pleased that your mother saved you from a lifetime of this by enrolling you at Orion. Oh, please don't mistake me. It's fun for a weekend of frivolity, but not quite a career path, now is it?"

"How now, fair maiden," Marq said, pouring on the charm in the direction of the headmaster's wife. "Thou be wedded to a fine gull and clumperton."

This made Mrs. Collins giggle and Headmaster Collins puff up. Clearly he thought he'd been complimented from the smooth way Marq had spoken. But I could tell by the expressions on Sam and Drea's faces that these were not exactly kind words.

"Aye, sir," Marq went on, knowing he was performing for two different audiences. "Thou art a moonling on a summer day."

"Why, thank you," Headmaster Collins said. He was beaming as if he could never imagine that anyone would be making fun of him. Must be nice to be that . . . unaware.

Mrs. Collins grabbed the headmaster by the arm and whispered something in his ear that caused his eyes to light up like she'd turned on a battery or something. This was never a good sign for the Orion Academy student body. The last time it happened, the headmaster got the bright idea that the school show should be double, triple, and in some cases quadruple cast to ensure everyone got a part of substance.

That didn't work out so well.

"Samantha, where can I find your mother?" the headmaster asked with an eagerness that scared us all.

"On the thither side of the faire by yon Tournament Arena at an establishment known to all as the House of Sandoval," Sam said, pointing him in the right direction. Mrs. Collins smiled with glee during the directions and smacked her husband, lovingly, on the bicep throughout the exchange.

"Best be off, swag," Sam added with a giggle.

"This is wonderful," he said. "See you all at the Back-to-School Picnic." The headmaster and his wife took off at a determined clip, leaving Sam, Marq, and Drea in riotous laughter, while the rest of us smiled, waiting for them to let us in on the joke. As I'd expected, every word they used had been an insult to our fair headmaster. Humorous indeed, but it would have been funnier if we'd all understood what was going on while it was happening.

The thing that worried me was what the headmaster's wife had whispered to him. Maybe they had been in on the joke and were planning to take it out on Sam by telling her mother? Either way, I didn't see anything good coming from that brief exchange.

"You do realize that the next item on the budget agenda for Orion Academy is going to be a collection of stocks for detention," I said. "Or maybe a functioning guillotine."

"He'd never get away with it," Hope said. "Parents would start sending their kids' chiropractor bills to the school in response. And it's *pillories*."

"Speaking of backs," I said. "Can someone please scratch mine?"

"I'll do it!" Marq said. How did I know that was going to happen? But, really, the itch was more uncomfortable than Marq helping with it, so I directed him to the spot behind my right shoulder blade and he took care of it nicely. Then, the scratch turned into something of a massage, which was weird and awkward, considering we'd only known each other for a few minutes. But it felt good, so I didn't say anything . . . until I saw Drew looking at us strangely.

"Okay, thanks," I said. "How much longer do I have to stay in this crazy contraption?" My hands were getting that tingly feeling like they were about to fall asleep. I slipped them through the wrist holes and shook them out, which was hard to do with my neck still encased in wood. All the shaking was causing me to rub more splinters into my skin.

"I think he's been up there long enough," Sam said, finally coming to my rescue. "I'm getting hungry, and he's going to be all whiny if we go off to eat without him."

My hero.

Once they finally let me out of the pillory, we broke for breakfast . . . or brunch, considering the time. It was a short walk to the food court, where more than a dozen stands were set up with a variety of foodstuffs. The choices ran to both ends of the spectrum from fried foods to healthy vegetarian options. There was little offered in between. Except the barrels of pickles, that is. So, we all split up to get what we wanted. Naturally, being the health-conscious person I am, I went with fish and chips and a funnel cake. Drew got an entire turkey leg that was supposed to be eaten King Henry the Eighth style. And the girls—and Marq—all ordered salads.

We reconvened by the salad stand—I *know*! I've never heard of a salad stand either—where the bulk of our group was picking up their orders. Drea slipped a buck into the tip jar, which earned her a bell ringing and a shout of "Huzzah to the tipper!" from the serving wench, which was a good enough reason for me to never tip anyone ever again. On the bright side, they didn't sing an obnoxious song like the people that worked at Coldstone Creamery.

Marq led us to a bench in the shade of a tree and we all dug in while Marq and Drea entertained us with more stories of their summer in the faire. Most of their tales were oddly interesting, from the one about the pet monkey that got loose in Sacramento to the yarn about the time the Commedia Players' costumes got lost in transit and they performed in their bloomers. I'd have thought Drea's story about becoming the youngest executioner in faire history would have been more . . . well, *more* . . . but she'd earned her position simply because her dad came in as the constable.

"We need to get moving if we're going to make *The Merry Wives of Whimsy*!" Marq exuded after he finished the rousing tale of the pilfered pirate booty. (Too hard to explain here, but let's just say that "booty" is a double entendre.)

Maybe it was because I'd been all caught up in his stories, but I agreed to go along without question. Because, really . . . *The Merry Wives of Whimsy?* That just begs questions, doesn't it?

The show was even more fun than I thought it would be. Three women dressed in aristocratic-type clothing performed bawdy slapstick comedy. Except for the bit with the audience participation—wherein I was doused with a bucketful of confetti—it quickly became the highlight of the day. Then again, considering my day thus far had consisted of public humiliation and starvation, that wasn't saying much.

A tip to the wise: If you're ever stuck at a Ren Faire, try to go with people in the know. Marq and Sam plotted out the entire day for us, making sure we caught the best shows in the bunch and using their connections to get us to the front of every line and priority seating for each event. Some of my more financially endowed school friends used to tell me they had something similar for VIP guests at Disneyland. I'd definitely have to try that sometime.

We followed up *Merry Wives* with *The Shakespeare Scholarzip,* which was a performance of all the bard's works in under one hour. Then, it was on to Da Vinci's Lecture on Modern Invention (circa 1500) for most of us, while Hope and Drea went off to hear an abridged retelling of the epic poem *Beowulf.* We reconvened later at an actual Renaissance Faire wedding, took a detour to boo the Queen's afternoon parade (because it made Marq happy), and ended the day at the

Tournament of Knights. I think the jousting and swordplay were a particular highlight for Drew. As evidenced by the bruise on my arm from all the times he punched me when something exciting happened.

All in all, it was an enjoyable way to spend the day considering where we were. Marq kept his knowing glances to a minimum and I forgot all about Sam's necklace at various points along the way. Which only made it more jarring when something would remind me. You'd be surprised how many references to unicorns you get during the course of a day at a Renaissance Faire. But every single one of them made me seethe a little more. Did she really think I was not going to notice that the necklace was gone? After what she had told me it meant?

I guess it wasn't in her plans to tell me, because the subject never managed to come up.

Several *hours* after we'd left, we returned to the House of Sandoval, where we were supposed to be helping out. Nobody minded that we'd been gone so long. In fact, Marq's mom told us she'd expected it to happen. Though it was surprising to learn that Anne had gone off to lunch with Jeremy and hadn't made her way back yet.

Hmmmmm.

"So, what can we do?" I asked.

"Um . . . nothing, actually," Sandy said. "Only people costumed in period clothes are supposed to work the booths. I hope you don't mind."

I looked to Drew, who was similarly attired in modernwear. "I don't mind. Do you mind?"

"Don't mind at all," he said, settling into a chair by the register that Hope quickly kicked out from under him. "What was *that* for?"

"If you're not working, you're certainly not resting while *we* work," she said.

"Then I might as well go home," Drew said, picking himself up off the ground.

"No," I said. "You can hang with me until we go. We're having movie night back at my—Sam, why are you giving me that look?"

"It's about . . . after," she said.

"What's about after what?" I asked.

Which was when Marq squealed. "The First Night Party!" He grabbed a flyer from behind the counter that announced the event that was spelled, "First Knight Party." (These Ren Faire folk do love their puns.) It was a celebration set for after the faire closed to the public. With the promise of a bonfire, the singing of bawdy songs, and more festive foods, it seemed entertaining enough. I'd wanted us to grab some takeout from Gladstone's and watch the entire line of Jaws movies while munching on seafood, but this was . . . well, not nearly as fun.

"See," I said, handing Drew the flyer, "if you leave now, you'll miss out on the festivit—why are you looking at me like that again, Sam?"

"I think this is why," Drew said, pointing to the bottom of the flyer.

It read: ALL THOSE BEDECKED IN PERIOD COSTUME ARE WEL-
COME. Translation: My Elizabethan cap wasn't going to cut it.
Blatant discrimination if you ask me.

"I'm sorry," Sam said. "I forgot all about First Knight."

"That's okay," I said, eyeing the rack of clothes nearest
me. It was our last weekend of fun before school started. I'd
intended to spend all of it with my friends. I'd already
enjoyed a lot of the faire. There was only one thing that
kept me from fully committing. All I had to do was put on
a silly costume. I'd certainly worn enough costumes onstage
over the years.

Yet, it was the one thing that I just couldn't do. Wearing
a costume onstage was one thing. Dressing up and running
around, playing some odd character . . . well, that crossed a
line in my book. Sort of the difference between being
adorably eccentric and crazy. Or the kind of thing that
made me different from Marq. Well, *one* of the things.

"Drew," I said, "can you give me a ride? My car's back at
Sam's."

"Sure," he replied.

I quickly said my "fare thee wells" before I guilted myself
into dressing up as a pirate or something.

I could have hung around for a while longer, but it would
have been all awkward while everyone else worked. Besides,
it would have just given Marq more of a chance to shoot me
questioning looks. Then I would have spent the rest of the
time trying not to shoot Sam questioning looks. All in all, it
was probably best that I left.

As Scarlet O'Hara so famously said, "Tomorrow is another day."

(Okay, I know that's Civil War era and not Renaissance. Don't be picky. They wore really big dresses in both periods.)

The Actor's Nightmare

Tomorrow might have been another day, but it was oddly reminiscent of the one before. At least this time I'd been smart enough to eat first. And to show up after the faire opened so I didn't have to go through the embarrassing costume check at the back entrance. The fifteen dollar entrance fee was so worth the lack of hassle. It did mean that I had to drive myself to the faire, which I didn't really mind. It was better to have an escape route with my car nearby in case boredom overwhelmed at some point. Drew had totally bailed on us and wouldn't be able to cart me home. I couldn't blame him. I *could* envy him. And I did.

The first thing on the agenda when I met up with my friends at the House of Sandoval was to check and see if Sam had her necklace back on. There was always a chance she had taken it off for some reason the day before. But if there had been some innocent reason on Friday, it was still true on

Saturday. Her neck was decidedly bare. I still wasn't sure how to bring it up, but we were going to have to talk about it at some point. I felt like there was this ticking clock on the conversation. Eric was coming back in two days and if we didn't address it now, I was pretty sure that we'd never talk about it. The fact that this particular ticking clock had Sam dressed in a wedding gown at the twelve o'clock hour was majorly freaking me out.

What? If you don't know by now that I have an overactive imagination, you haven't been paying attention.

Sam, however, seemed to be totally oblivious to the clock or to my repeated glances in the direction of her neck. Unless it was all an act and she knew that I knew what she did. She is one of the most talented actresses I've ever met. An innocent act is the same whether or not she's onstage. But why would she need to act around me?

I finally worked up my determination to confront her when she shut me down before I could even open my mouth.

"I swear I'm going to make this up to you," she said. Never a good opening line.

"What now?" I asked, bracing myself.

Then she went and looked all sheepish. "Since we didn't really help the Sandovals out all that much yesterday," she said, "I wanted to stick around for a couple hours this morning. I would have called you—"

"But nobody here has a cell phone on them," I finished her thought. I couldn't imagine what these people did in an emergency. I was *so* not meant to live in pre-industrial times.

"You can go and explore the faire on your own, if you want," she said. "You don't have to stick around and watch us work."

"That's okay," I said, pulling a paperback book out of my back pocket. "I came prepared." Without another word, I left the tent and headed for a quiet patch of shade beneath a tree to get in some last-minute summer reading. Considering the reading was for Anne's class, I felt that I was doing my part.

Not that I could concentrate on *Fahrenheit 451* when I had other burning issues on my mind. Namely: why didn't Sam feel like she could talk to me? And why—if this was our last big weekend before school started—was I spending so much of it alone? And why didn't I sleep in and come to the faire later? That last one was really bothering me while I turned the pages. It was bothering me so much that my body decided to answer it for me by falling asleep with the book in my lap.

What? Like I had anything better to do?

I was in the middle of a ridiculously easy to decipher dream where I was being chased by rainbow colored unicorns when something banged against my foot. I snorted awake to find that it was Hope's foot. "Come on," she said.

I rubbed the sleep from my eyes, got up, and followed. "And we're going where?" I asked.

"Someplace you can help without being in costume," she said. "Or, I should say, where you don't have to be entirely in costume." It took me a second to figure out what she meant. Then I noticed the new addition to my wardrobe. Oh, I was still in my fedora. But, while I was sleeping, Sandy managed to slip this cool leather pouch onto my belt. Even better, when I opened it, I found a tin of dark chocolate covered Altoids inside. The perfect thing for my post-nap breath. I popped one in my mouth and offered one to Hope. "Am I going to like this whatever it is we're doing?" I asked.

"Highly doubtful," she said taking the mint.

The next logical question would be, why would I do it? But since I already knew the answer to that one—because Hope was telling me to—I decided to leave it unasked. Besides, as we've already established, I had more pressing questions on my mind.

The main question at the moment was whether or not Sam had confided in Hope about sleeping with Eric. I couldn't imagine that she would have. Hope had been in New York until the middle of the week. If Sam couldn't talk to me about it in person, I doubted that she'd pick up a phone and call all the way to New York. Right?

But it was worth trying to find out. Naturally, I couldn't just up and ask her. I had to be subtle about this. "I wonder what's going to happen when Eric gets home? You think him and Sam are going to keep dating or he's going to dump her?"

That was me being subtle. Sad, isn't it?

"How should I know?" Hope said, confirming everything I was hoping she wouldn't. Mind you, it wasn't *what* she said. It was what she didn't. This subject would normally send us into a gossip spiral until we examined every possible ramification of the return of Eric in Sam's life, our lives, and the lives of everyone in our social circle. "How should I know?" was intended to do just the opposite. She was try-ing to shut me down.

Like that was going to work.

I stopped and looked Hope over for a second. Being Hope, she didn't avert her eyes and shy away from me. She looked me dead on. A challenge.

I took a risk and decided to be direct for a change. "She told you."

"Told me what?" Hope asked, still looking straight at me.

"About her and Eric," I said.

"About her and Eric . . . *what?*" she asked.

"Why are you pulling attitude with me?" I asked.

"Because I told Sam this would happen."

"Aha!" I blurted out, pointing a finger up to the sky like I was a lawyer on some classic legal drama who had just forced a witness to reveal that she was the killer. "So you *admit* that Sam and Eric had sex!"

"Take it down a notch," Hope said, making sure no one around us was listening to our conversation. "There are ears all over this place. And, no, I admitted nothing."

"Oh, come on," I said in a low voice. "You know that I know. Why can't you just tell me and get it over with."

"And what do you plan to do if I tell you?" she asked.

"Confront Sam."

"*Confront* Sam?" she asked. "Really. What gives you the right to confront Sam about it? About anything, really?"

"I'm her best friend," I reminded Hope. Then dialed it back, remembering who I was talking to. "One of her best friends.

Why would she keep something like that from me?" Really. I wanted an answer.

"You know, Drew's stuff is as good as this," Hope said, turning her attention to a cart with charcoal sketches of romantic couples through the ages: Romeo and Juliet, Antony and Cleopatra, Dracula and Mina. Her comment was quite the non sequitur.

"What are you talking about?" I asked.

"Drew's drawings," Hope said as she started walking again. "He could totally sell his stuff here."

"Drew's doing his art again?" I asked, following her through the crowd. This was news to me. Drew had put down his pencils back when soccer—and Eric—took over his life. Growing up, he was a really talented artist. His work could make the ugliest refrigerator look like a high-end gallery. But, like so many things, he seemed to grow out of it.

"He sent me some sketches over the summer," Hope said.

Funny how Drew and I had been hanging out all that time and he never mentioned it. Even funnier was how I was letting Hope distract me from the conversation at hand.

"Getting back to the subject," I said.

But Hope cut me off for good with a "Here he is."

I groaned when I realized where we were. Drea was pulling day two of dungeon duty up on the platform with a pair of hardened criminals in gaudy Hawaiian shirts locked in the stocks . . . I mean, pillory. "I wasn't on my cell phone," I protested.

"Not that," Hope said. "Drea got the guillotine working

last night. "She needs a civilian volunteer for the noon beheading."

"Me?" I asked.

I got my answer when Drea came over to us and said, "Thanks for this, Bryan. I didn't want to risk testing out the guillotine on some unsuspecting tourist with his family watching."

"Test?" I asked. "You mean you're not sure that it's working?"

"No!" Drea said. "It's working. I did a couple practice runs with some cantaloupe. Three out of four of those went well." I was praying that the smile she threw in Hope's direction meant she was joking.

I shot my own glance at Hope that told her that not only would I get her back for this, but I would also be continuing our conversation at a later time.

The glare she shot back was much more concise. It told me to get over it.

I filed "it" away while Drea walked me through the guillotine trick once before taking me behind the platform to put me in shackles. She then announced to the gathering crowd that it was time for the noon beheading. This was apparently some kind of ceremonial thing, so it took a while to go through the motions before I was dragged out in front of everyone to play my part. This time, someone did actually throw a tomato at me. It was hollow plastic, but annoying all the same.

Drea placed my head in the guillotine then proceeded to list off my make believe crimes. I didn't understand what half of them were, but by the end even I thought I was a bad, bad person. Drea asked me if I had any last words, but before I could come up with anything, I heard the whistle of the blade and a thud as everything went black.

Don't worry. I'm not narrating from the grave. The trick guillotine worked, and my head—with body still attached—dropped into the bucket. Following the applause, I waited while Hope held up a curtain to hide the removal of my body and Drea released me from the machine.

"Thanks," she said. "You really freaked out the kids."

"Well then, I've met my goal for the day," I said. "It was fun. Much better than getting locked up in that thing again." I pointed over to the pillory.

Little did I know that I'd find myself locked up again not four hours later. . . .

"What did he do now?" Hope asked as she joined us back at the "dungeon." A small leather journal was hanging round her neck and she was making notes in it with a pencil made from a twig. She'd managed to avoid the rest of our conversation earlier by spending the afternoon helping Drea on dungeon duty before making a quick exit to find something to write on when I refused to let her use my phone again. Too bad I couldn't resist the temptation myself.

"Same as yesterday," Marq said with actual glee. "Anachronistic technology!"

"I read a text message from Suze," I said, hunched over in the stocks . . . I mean pillory. "But I didn't text her back! And

I'm not wearing the cap!" I was hoping they didn't notice the pouch on my belt.

"Which is why you only get fifteen minutes in here today," Drea said.

Sam was standing off to the side being amused, but knowing better than to say anything. I was a good sport and all, but we were getting pretty close to that line where I'd stop playing along.

In fact, we were about to cross it.

"And what do we have here?" a disarmingly genteel voice asked. I didn't have to see above the rim of my fedora to recognize that well-rehearsed innocent act. Holly Mayflower had come to the faire. And judging from the cold front that just came through, she was not alone.

I lifted my head to see Holly standing alongside Hope's evil stepsisters, Alexis and Belinda.

Together again.

Holly had cheated her way into a spot at one of the foremost acting schools in the country at the start of summer. The good news was that it took her to New York for two blissful months. The bad news was that she came home at the end. Considering that she probably just got back, I had trouble imagining that the Renaissance Faire was tops on her itinerary. She and the steps were the last three people I'd expected to see at the faire. Besides myself, that is. Even more surprising was that they had all gotten into the spirit of things. Sort of.

Holly and Belinda were each dressed in peasant dresses of blue and cream respectively. Just to be clear, they weren't dressed as peasants. They were in very modern, very reveal-ing outfits that were probably bought in one of the most expensive stores in town. Certainly not something they'd picked up at the House of Sandoval. It wasn't close to being actually in costume, but it was closer than I was ever going to get, Sandy's accessories notwithstanding.

Alexis, however, was—as the great and wondrous fashion maven, Tim Gunn would say—a hot mess. Clearly, she'd mixed up her Renaissance with her Ancient Greece and was decked out in what could only be called a toga. It was a toga in silk with real gold accents, but a toga nonetheless.

And it was *awesome*.

Where I succeeded in choking back the laughter, my friends failed miserably. Largely because they didn't care if the evil trio knew they were being laughed at. Marq and Drea laughed along, not quite knowing why they were laughing, but going along in the spirit of friendship.

"What are you doing here?" Sam asked the obvious ques-tion once she'd caught her breath.

"Taking in the sights," Holly replied. For some reason I was the sight in her sights when she replied. "And what did you do to get put in there? Crimes against fashion with that stupid hat?"

I felt an overwhelming urge to Hulk out and burst from the pillory. Nobody messes with the fedora. But since I couldn't even *attempt* to smash my bonds, or come up with a witty retort, I just dropped my head and ignored her.

"No, seriously," Sam said. "I thought you never went anywhere that didn't have a thirty dollar cover charge and a line of paparazzi outside the front door. What brings you to this neck of the condemned golf course? There *has* to be a reason."

"You know me too well," Holly replied.

"Unfortunately," Sam said.

Holly cracked the gum in her mouth and twirled her red hair like she was a fifties bad girl or something. I was worried she was going to hurt herself by straddling too many time periods at once. "I was talking with Headmaster Collins at dinner last night," Holly said.

"You often dine with the headmaster?" Hope asked. That would explain so much about how the Mayflowers got away with things.

"It was Heather's good-bye dinner," Holly explained, refer- ring to her almost-as-evil big sister. "He was a big help making sure she didn't lose her spot at Princeton after the unfortunate events of the school show last year."

"Anyway," Sam said, waving her hand in a circular motion, prompting Holly to move along. Only Holly would refer to her sister's sabotage of the school play that could have resulted in at least one charge of attempted murder as "unfor- tunate events." But why quibble with semantics? I was sure she was about to give us a lot more to quibble over.

"Anyway," Holly repeated with a nod, "he was telling us all about the Renaissance Faire and how he talked to the organiz- ers about coming out for the Back-to-School Picnic on Mon- day. You know, bringing some of these loony faire people to perform. Maybe do some of their quaint acts or whatever."

So that she and her friends could make fun of them, I thought.

"These loony faire people are my friends," Sam said.

As one, the trio of terror turned and looked Drea up and down like she was something on the bottom of their Ferragamos. Drea's executioner robes weren't exactly flattering to her shape. They actually made her look kind of rectangular. And the sneer on Holly's face was enough of a comment when she got to Marq.

Hope's fists were clenching at her sides, while Sam and Drea each took a step down from the platform so they were all lined up in a nice little row facing down Holly and the steps. It was like they were preparing to reenact a scene from *West Side Story*. Without the dancing.

"Oh no, honey," Marq said, stepping in between the two trios. "We do not have throw-downs at the Ren Faire. Save that for the Galleria."

Holly and Alexis clearly didn't know what to make of Marq, but I thought I saw Belinda covering her mouth to hide a laugh. Either way, the tension dropped a notch, which is good because I doubt there was a Ren Faire phrase for "cat fight."

"Which brings us back to what you're doing here," Sam said.

"He put me in charge of everything," Holly said. This, I took to mean that she didn't book that guest role on the medical drama du jour. Pity. "And he's asked me to perform a skit. In true Renaissance fashion," she continued. "Show off some of what I learned in Blackstone's acting program this summer." Her smile was doing a good job hiding the knife she was twisting into Sam's gut. They had been each other's main competition for that spot in the acting program. Holly had won out based on her impressive acting talent and her daddy's more than impressive wallet.

"You're going to put this all together by yourself in two days?" I asked.

"Well, the faire people are just going to swing by and, like, juggle for us or whatever. It's the skit that's going to be the hard part. But, I've enlisted Belinda to work on it with me," Holly said. "And I asked Jason and Gary, too. They are the best actors in the school. Alexis is going to do costumes. I'm sure we can find something for you all to do."

"Just not with the costumes," Alexis said. "Seeing how they're dressed now, I don't think they'll be much help." This from the one about a thousand years off in her wardrobe choice. And I was the one being punished for an anachronism.

As I braced for a wench fight, our savior came in the form of Anne, who was walking, with purpose, right toward us. She was also walking with Jeremy. And I swear that when I first saw them out of the corner of my eye they were holding hands.

By the time Anne and Jeremy reached us, placing themselves physically between the two camps, there was no sign of recent handholding developments. Not that anyone other than me would have noticed if there were. The glaring contest was in full effect.

"Holly," Anne said, "welcome back. How was New York?"

"Wonderful," Holly said, without taking her eyes off Sam. "I never imagined how unprepared we were at Orion. I mean, Mr. Randall's a great drama teacher and all, but he's no Hartley Blackstone. That man's a genius."

"Well, congratulations," Anne said with a smoothness that comes from years of teaching the pampered children of the pampered Hollywood elite. "I'm sure you made the most of the experience. And I hear that you're ready to jump right back into acting at Orion and our little Renaissance Faire world too."

"You know me," Holly said. "Full of school spirit."

Sam leaned over to Hope and said in a whisper that carried, "More like full of—"

"Headmaster Collins called me last night to tell me about your kind offer to help us plan the events for Monday," Anne quickly interjected.

Help us? That sounded somewhat different from Holly's story where she was in charge of the whole thing.

"I think the idea of student-performed skits is wonderful," Anne continued. I felt like I was in the presence of a master. She may be a teacher, but Holly's parents had the power to get Anne in a lot of trouble if she'd ever hurt their precious daughter's feelings. It was like watching the work of a true artiste as Anne deftly put Holly in her place. "I suggested— and Headmaster Collins agreed—that *two* skits would be perfect for the picnic. That way, we can show this world as seen through the eyes of a novice, such as yourself, and by people more familiar with the Renaissance-era style of performance. Led by Sam, of course." Anne finished with her hand on her daughter's shoulder.

"A great idea," Holly said, smiling through her pain.

"Certainly, we'll be happy to help out any way we can," Anne offered.

"Definitely," Sam added. "I'm sure there's a lot of things that Holly doesn't understand."

That earned Sam a look of reproach from her mom. "Why don't we start with costumes," Anne said. "If you three come with me, we have some friends with a costume shop."

"That's okay," Alexis said, "I was thinking—"

"Nonsense," Anne said. I wondered if she meant that the idea of Alexis "thinking" was nonsense, but I didn't say anything. "My friends have already agreed to give all the students a discount." Somehow, I suspected that "discount" would be to mark up the price. "You three, come with us."

We all watched as Anne and Jeremy led Holly and her minions off to the House of Sandoval and out of our hair. At least, for the moment.

Gypsy

"What was *that*?" Marq asked.

"Holly," Sam, Hope, and I said in unison, as if that explained it all. Funny how we did that about Marq earlier too.

Since the name alone didn't really touch on the shallow depths of Holly Mayflower, Sam quickly filled Marq and Drea in on the history. She started all the way back to Sam's first week at Orion when our drama teacher, Mr. Randall, made the fateful mistake of complimenting Sam and Holly on a scene they were assigned together. He said that they were the most perfect pairing he'd ever seen. Rather than creating a friendship and acting partnership, as I can only assume our teacher had intended, he unknowingly let loose a rivalry that rivals *The Rivals*. (*Aside:* That's a play by Richard Brinsley Sheridan. It's a comedy of manners that doesn't entirely fit in the context, but I like how it rounds out the sentence, so go with it.)

Once Sam had explained Holly, Hope threw in a few lines

about her wicked stepsisters just so Marq and Drea had the full picture . . . in HD even. Considering it looked like we were going to be locked in *another* battle of us against them, it was best that they understood the enemy.

Not that anyone would ever *truly* understand Holly Mayflower.

Once the tales were told, Marq nodded his head all contemplatively. "We are going to kick their asses."

"Yes!" Drea said.

No, I thought. The last thing we needed was a repeat of the dueling scenes that we'd performed at the start of summer. I was not up for ending the summer with another rendition of So You Think You Can Act? Even if this time the stakes would be lower. There was already too much drama for the last weekend of summer, if you ask me.

"Hold it," I said, throwing my head back so I could see everyone. Unfortunately, I'd forgotten where I was and slammed the back of my skull into the wooden bar that held me in place, knocking my fedora off in the process. "Will someone get me out of this thing? Now!"

"Okay, okay," Drea said. She slipped the rusty skeleton key into the oversized lock. I heard a click and felt the wooden bar being lifted on its hinge, followed by a warm breeze on the back of my neck. Freedom.

I stood up and stretched my back. "Much better. Now about this skit-off. Clearly, we're going to be better than Holly and the Hollettes. You guys have been doing this Ren Faire stuff forever. So why don't we just have fun, play around with the skit, and not worry about anyone else for once? I'm not in the mood to turn this into another round of us versus the Mayflower power. Who's with me?"

My friends all stood stupefied for a moment. It wasn't like me to not care about a challenge. But, really, it was our last weekend of summer freedom and we were nowhere near having the kind of laid back enjoyment I'd been hoping for.

Marq was the first one to speak. "Kick their collective asses from here to the Dark Ages!"

"Still in!" Drea said.

I looked to Sam for an assist. She'd already chosen her faire friends the night before. Now it was time to listen to me.

Thankfully, she chose wisely.

This time.

"No," she said, "Bryan's right. Let's just have fun. I want to show Bryan and Hope what Ren Faire life is really like. Kicking Holly's ass is not the goal here." She smiled. "It's just an added bonus. Marq, think of this as a way of prepping yourself to get back into maneuvering through the high school social setting. You don't always have to go in for the kill. Sometimes, just being better than your enemies is enough."

This was not the time to remind Marq that, after a year of home schooling, he would be reentering the world of structured torment when he started attending an actual high school in a few days. Upon that realization, he dramatically collapsed at the knees. I guess Sam and Drea were used to it, because they didn't even react, whereas Hope and I both jumped.

"School," he repeated woozily, with the back of his hand pressed against his forehead. He laid out on the stage like he was performing the death scene from some overwrought, tragic drama. "The bourgeois life. Or, as the French say, *la vie bourgeois.*"

"Are you okay?" I asked.

"Hardly," he said. "Being reminded that this is my last weekend of freedom." Heavy sigh. "It overwhelms."

"We get it, drama queen," Sam said.

"Get what?" I asked. I wasn't getting anything at all. I mean, sure, I haven't been homeschooled for the past year, but this was the last weekend of my summer freedom and I wasn't getting the vapors or anything.

"He wants to go to WeHo," Sam explained.

Marq perked up right quick. I didn't know how we went from Holly Mayflower to WeHo, but I was more confused by why he needed to put on an act, instead of just asking us. WeHo wasn't on *my* top ten list of things to do the last weekend before school started, but it wasn't the end of the world, or anything. (*Aside:* WeHo . . . better known as West Hollywood . . . also known as Boy Town . . . is the gay capital of the L.A. area. Clubs, restaurants, bookstores—and *those kinds* of bookstores—fill the little city that tends to triple its population on the weekends.)

"I *like* it," Drea said. "I read in the *LA Weekly* that Book Soup is having a lesbian poetry night."

Marq looked like he had been burned. "Hmmm . . . a night of bitter rants against men? That is *so* not on the list." Wow. I always find it interesting when people who act like major stereotypes start trashing other people's stereotypes. You know?

Although, in all honesty, I wasn't up for lesbian poetry night either. Or any poetry night, really.

"Well, that's what I'm doing," Drea said. "Hope, why don't you come with me? It could be fun."

"Sure," Hope said, after brief consideration.

Drea threw an arm around Hope. "That's settled. Sam?"

I'll give Sam credit. She politely made it look like she was thinking the options over, but Sam was as into poetry as I was. Besides, I knew she wouldn't blow off her GBF. "I'm with Marq."

"Fab!" Marq said. "Then Sam, Bry, and I will hit Santa Monica Boulevard for some ribald debauchery, while you two explore the dark side of feminist lit on Sunset." He sprung up from the ground and wrapped his arms around me and Sam like we'd just picked teams for some sport or something.

Odd how no one asked me if I'd even wanted to go to WeHo. And just like in school, I was picked last. Even at the Ren Faire I can't catch a break.

"Now that that's settled," Sam said. "We need to figure out a skit. Hope, what have you got?"

Hope looked offended. "I can't just create on command," she said, even though we'd both seen her do just that on numerous occasions. "I've got other things on my mind right now." Sam and I shared a glance, wondering what exactly was on Hope's mind. It wasn't like her to pass up an opportunity to create drama.

Wait. That sounds wrong.

"What we need"—Marq said, with a pause for dramatic effect—"is inspiration. And we all know where the best place to find inspiration for a skit is."

Well, no, we *all* didn't know.

"Rosencrantz & Guildenstern's!" Marq, Drea, and Sam cheered.

Yeah. Still wasn't getting it. But I played along. "I thought they were dead." (*Aside:* That's a theater joke. Actually, it's more like a *theatre* joke. Related to a Tom Stoppard play, which is related to Shakespeare's *Hamlet*. Look it up if you don't get it.)

"Funny," Marq said as he squeezed me closer to his body. "Come!" He kept me and Sam in a headlock as we went off toward the far end of the faire with Drea and Hope bringing up the rear.

I thought it was difficult the day before when he'd grabbed me by the back of my shirt and pulled me, backward, through the faire, but this was ridiculous. We kept tripping over one another and stumbling as we walked.

"Marq," Sam said, "release!" And he listened.

Once we were free, Sam and I dropped back and we all shifted position. Now, Marq and Drea led us to wherever it was we were going, and Hope stayed behind, scribbling in her little journal as she followed.

"And what," I asked Sam, "*is* Rosencrantz & Guildenstern's?"

"Prop shed," she explained. "Anything and everything you would need to put on a skit, from slap sticks to trick swords."

"So you want to buy the props before we know what kind of skit we're doing?"

"Borrow," Sam corrected. "And what else can we do when our writer seems to be off in another world. Don't worry. It'll be fun."

Oh, but I was worried. But not about the props. I was a tad nervous about the skit and, specifically, what they thought my role in the skit was going to be. The last time I'd been onstage at Orion Academy it was—to be blunt—a nightmare of epic proportions.

Then again, improv skits aren't serious acting. Improvisation is a difficult talent to master, but you can usually fall back on playing an exaggerated version of yourself to get by. As long as I kept my part to a minimum—which seemed likely with this collection of hams—I'd be fine. But I still wasn't planning on wearing the tights. That was a deal breaker.

As Marq and Drea hurried ahead of us and Hope dragged behind, I realized I was alone with Sam for the first time since I'd figured out that she was keeping something from me. The middle of the Ren Faire wasn't the best time for the conversation, but I couldn't help but be tempted. It wasn't even that I wanted to talk about her doing the deed. I was much more interested in finding out why she didn't want to talk to me about it.

But I got distracted when I'd suddenly lost Marq and Drea. Largely because they're not an easy pair to lose, considering how they were skipping . . . and singing a drinking song about some guy named Finnegan. Loudly.

"Where did—"

"This way," Sam pulled me aside to go down what could only be called a dark and scary alleyway. I'd been at the faire for a day and a half and I never noticed this little side street that broke off from the last row and went into the trees. The shadows around us, the darkened tents, and the general disreputable look of the people around us gave it the feel of Knockturn Alley from Harry Potter. Here were the carts selling bongs and pot pipes. Signs proudly proclaimed traders in black magic and dark mojo. A green fairy pointed the way into a tent I could only assume was a dive bar where one could purchase some absinthe.

Kind of figures this would be where the theater stuff would be located.

Questions about this dark side of the Ren Faire were on the tip of my tongue, when a withered old woman sprang out at us from beside her cart. Okay, maybe *sprang* is a bit of hyperbole. But she was somehow, suddenly, in our path raising a wrinkled hand toward us. "Death to all those who pass without bidding fair greeting."

I looked past the hag, hoping to see Marq and Drea, but they were long gone. As I considered throwing Sam at the woman and running for my life, a laugh and a squeal came from my intended shield.

"Florella!" Sam said. "I can't believe you're here!"

I remained tense, ready to flee as Sam wrapped the frail woman in a hug I was pretty sure was going to snap her bones.

"Two days," the woman said as she hugged back. "Two days of festivities, and this is the first I see you, child."

I could see the backs of Sam's ears going red. "I'm sorry, Flor, but I didn't think you were traveling with the faire anymore."

"Heard I was dead again, huh?" the woman said as she released Sam. "So many people trying to do me in before my time. They should look so good if my age they reach." Not only did she look like Yoda, now the woman was sounding like the green guy too. I worried that she was going to bust out some mean kung fu force moves on us if we disrespected her. Sam laughed a nervous laugh and introduced me in a clear attempt to divert the conversation.

I held out my hand and she grabbed it, pulling me toward her cart. "Come," she said. "Buy your girlfriend a nice trinket."

"She's not my girlfriend," I corrected out of habit. Sam and I get that a lot. Well, not when she is attached to Eric all the time. But since he'd been gone for most of the summer, we'd been hearing it again.

"What? She is not a girl?" Florella asked. "She is not a friend? Do boys only buy gifts now for girls who show them their breasts?"

"Flor!" Sam gasped as my eyes rolled into the back of my head.

Florella gave a half laugh as she stuck a silver butterfly pendant into my hands. "This one always liked the butterflies," she said with a nod in Sam's direction. "Or fairies. Fairies are always good. And wizards. Such power in wizards . . . but I think not for Sam. No. Possibly a dragon to match the fire in her spirit." Florella eyed Sam as she changed out pendants with surprising swiftness that I wouldn't have expected from someone who had to be at least two centuries old. "Yes, a dragon. I've known this girl all her life and the dragon is a perfect match for her personality."

For some reason, Sam looked offended. I'm sure I just looked confused. Part of that confusion was because I honestly didn't know what to make of Florella. The other part came from not knowing how to respond. With silver necklaces being switched in and out of my hands with alarming speed, it was getting increasingly difficult to ignore the one necklace missing from the equation.

It became *way* harder to ignore when Florella pointed it out to us.

"You've stopped wearing my necklace, I see," Florella said to Sam. "My unicorn necklace," she added, destroying any chance we had of pretending she wasn't talking about what she was talking about. "I made that necklace special for her many moons ago," she said to me. "Never took it off, did she? Until now. Probably lost it."

Or lost *something*, I thought. But I couldn't say it. Not there. Not then.

Not until Florella hurried off to accost another potential customer.

"So, did you lose it?"

"No," she replied, tensely. "I know where it is."

"And who you gave it to," I added with full snark.

Then she decided to play all dumb. "I don't know what you're talking about." Which was pure bull. Even with her fine acting ability, no one would have bought that line read. Not that it mattered, because Hope finally caught up to us, saw us by the necklaces, took in the situation, and blew all pretense out of the water.

"I didn't tell him," Hope said as *everyone's* attention rested squarely at the base of Sam's neck. "He guessed it on his own."

"Yeah, but you just *confirmed* it," Sam said.

"She didn't have to confirm anything," I said, a tad more loudly than I'd intended. "And she didn't need to tell me anything, either. You did. Back when you told me what the necklace meant to you. I just want to know why you couldn't tell me—"

"We're *not* doing this here," Sam said, indicating the small crowd of darkly dressed faire people who had stopped to listen. Even in my agitated state, I knew better than to continue this discussion in a place where we'd become the talk of the faire, and word could potentially get back to Anne.

But I wasn't entirely ready to give up on it either. "Where?" I said. "And when?"

"Nowhere and never," Sam replied as she stomped off to join Marq and Drea, with a derisive snort in Hope's direction.

"Don't pin this on me," Hope shouted after her.

"What the hell was that about?" I asked.

"Couldn't leave it alone, could you?" Hope said.

Wait. When did I become the bad guy in this? I wasn't the one keeping secrets. I wasn't the one talking behind my best friend's back. BF, GBF, or whatever label we put on it, we were supposed to be beyond that. A fact that I pointed out to Hope.

"Some things are private," Hope said.

"From me?" I said. "Anything else you two hiding?"

"Can't you just let her have this?" Hope asked. "Can't you just ignore it?"

"Yes, I could," I said. "But why should I? Sam was the one who told me about the necklace. She *wanted* me to know. And now that I do know, she acts like it's not my business. Friends don't keep secrets."

If it means anything, I can freely admit that I fully knew at the time that I was being a hypocrite.

A Little Night Music

Night was falling. Summer was ending. The leaves . . .
okay, that's about as far as I can go with the whole "last weekend before school" imagery. In other parts of the country I
could talk about the bursts of colors on the soon-to-be chang-
ing leaves and the brisk air, but not in Malibu, where the sun
had just dipped beneath the Pacific and I hadn't even brought
a light jacket along for the evening. Labor Day was nearly
upon us and the unofficial end of summer was even more unofficial here as I turned off the Pacific Coast Highway and pulled
into the main parking lot of Pepperdine University.

The school had rented out a couple spots on the campus to
the gypsy Ren Faire folk to set up their RVs and mobile homes
while the faire was in town. It was only a short trip down a
windy road to the country club where the faire was. This was
also the satellite lot for the guest overflow parking, so it took
me a few minutes to navigate through the cars and shuttle

buses back to the much quieter lot where the makeshift city was housed.

I parked at the end of a row of empty spots along the gated area where the mobile homes had set up their little town. The faire was still in full swing, so it wasn't a surprise that I was pretty much by myself in this part of the lot. A lone security guy was stationed at the entrance to the temporary trailer park. Thankfully, he was dressed in typical security uniform, not Renaissance costume, so I didn't expect any attitude about my wardrobe.

I told the guard my name and he checked it against his guest list. Apparently, the faire folk had suffered some collegiate pranks since setting up camp and now access to the mini city was restricted to residents and their guests. I guess the guard found what he was looking for, because he let me pass with a welcome nod, even offering a map to the lot so that I could find the Sandoval's place. I took the map, but I didn't wind up using it. Marq had already provided incredibly detailed directions, noting landmarks like "the red RV that looks like a harlot's boudoir—both inside *and* out" and "the VW van that reeks of pot from two rows away." After a few more colorful descriptions, I found the surprisingly nondescript trailer with the sign THE MOBILE HOUSE OF SANDOVAL outside.

I knocked on the door to the Sandoval trailer and braced myself for what I was about to experience. And not just the part about seeing Sam. We hadn't talked much since our brief exchange over the necklace. A few grunts about prop choices and generic nothingness on the way back to the Sandovals' tent had been the sum total of our conversational abilities that afternoon. We'd managed to be civil while we made arrangements to meet at Marq's trailer after I headed home to change. But seeing Sam again wasn't the reason for the tension I felt. Well, not the *entire* reason.

Considering Marq had been dressed as a queen—I mean, *the* queen—when I first met him, I wasn't sure what his preferred style of dress for a night in West Hollywood would be. Flamboyant? That was a given. But would it be gender specific, gender neutral, or gender blender?

My fears proved largely unfounded when Marq opened the door dressed in tight black jeans that accentuated his sticklike legs, a Target-style faux vintage T, and a bunch of silver jewelry. Not only was it subdued, but it was kind of like what I was wearing, except my jeans weren't as tight, my shirt was genuine vintage, and the only accessories I wore were a watch and my usual fedora.

It wasn't until I stepped inside and into the light that I saw his nails were painted. And I don't mean a cool color like blue, black, or vamp red. No. These nails were pink. Or maybe coral. But probably the true name on the bottle was something like Princess Shimmer or Strawberry Sorbet.

It looked kind of fey, if you ask me. Not that I was being judgmental.

Me? *Never!*

"You found me!" he squealed, wrapping me in a big, bony hug while I prayed that those nails were dry. I quickly shoved my face into his shoulder so that he couldn't try to kiss me in what was proving to be his preferred manner of greeting. I think I may have chipped a tooth on his sharp bony-ness.

"Yeah," I said, pulling away. "Your directions were spot on. I think I reek of pot, and I didn't even get near that VW."

"It lingers," he warned, then insisted on giving me the grand tour. Being that we were in an RV, it was a quick trip. The Sandovals had made the most out of a tight living situation. Sandy's clothing patterns and materials were scattered all around in neatly organized piles. The place was fairly homey, considering. Family pictures were stuck to the walls, hand-sewn curtains covered the windows, and there was even a beanbag chair next to the puffy little couch. All in all, I could see the Sandovals living happily together in the tight quarters.

That laid-back lifestyle took on an entirely different picture when I imagined myself living in a similar situation with my own parents. Our house wasn't exactly one of the big mansions at the top of the mountains, but I truly valued having a bedroom with a door I could close to shut out the world.

"I like it," I said when we finished the brief tour. "Nice and cozy."

"And it gets way cozier when we have parties with a few dozen of our closest friends," Marq said. "A friendly game of twister can turn deadly when you've only got four feet of floor space." I got claustrophobic just thinking about it.

"Is Sam on her way?" I asked. It wasn't like her to be late. Usually she was way early for any event.

For the first time since I met him, Marq seemed . . . shy?

"Um," he said, haltingly. "Well . . . she kind of . . . she sort of bailed."

"*What?*" That sounded way harsher than I'd intended it. You know, considering I realized it was just going to be Marq and me. I didn't want him to think I was horrified that I had to spend time with him. But I couldn't stop myself from being upset with Sam for ditching. And, in all honesty, being alone with him did make me a wee bit nervous. "When? Why?"

If Marq was shy before, he was absolutely embarrassed now. "There was a message for me when I got home. She said something suddenly came up."

Wow. Not only did she bail, she didn't even bother to come up with an excuse. It must have been a mighty sudden something, considering it could only have taken a few minutes from the time they parted at the faire to when Marq got home. But that didn't explain why she didn't call me, too. I had my cell phone on me the whole time, so it wasn't like she couldn't track me down.

No matter how I looked at it—and I was considering standing on my head to get a different perspective on things—Sam was avoiding me. ME! This was unprecedented. Sure, we've been known to ignore one another from time to time. We've both been caught in rogue depressions where we wanted to shut out the entire world. But this was different. This wasn't a rogue depression. This was one of those life moments specifically created for sharing with your best friend.

On top of that, we *never* used intermediaries with lame excuses. We never bailed on plans. We never did any of this.

I slumped down in the beanbag chair wondering what was going on with her. And with us. This left an awful big silence in an awful small RV.

"I guess you're going to bail on me too?" Marq asked.

I felt like I'd just kicked a puppy. A puppy with pretty, pretty pink fingernails, which, honestly, made me feel worse. The crazy thing was, I hadn't actually done anything. Sure, I briefly thought about canceling when I found out Sam wasn't coming, but I didn't say it out loud.

Marq had been so excited about going to WeHo. Not that "excited" wasn't his natural state, but there had been a considerable increase in his bounciness since we came up with the plan. To be honest, I'd been buzzed about it too. It *was* the last weekend of summer, and I was looking to celebrate it in some way that didn't require tunics and tights.

Although, in West Hollywood, you never knew what you'd see.

"No," I said, forcing a smile. "I'm still in. I just . . . I didn't know she wasn't coming. But that doesn't mean we can't have fun in WeHo ourselves."

I guess Marq took my general mood to mean something different than it did. "We can even have more fun now. I mean, who needs girls in Boy Town, anyway? And now we can be totally free to *be*. You don't have to worry at all. Whatever happens in WeHo stays in WeHo. I'm not going to say a thing."

"About what?" I asked, genuinely clueless.

"You know," he said with a nod.

I honestly did not.

"About . . . ," he started. "Oh my God! You do know, don't you?"

The first thing that popped into my mind was that he was talking about Sam. In my defense, that was already in my mind, so it wasn't much of a leap. And let me tell you, I was plenty mad that she had confided in him what she refused to confirm to me. It didn't matter that he knew her first or even that he knew her longer. I knew her *now*!

"I kind of sussed it out," I said, in what I can only hope was an adorably clueless manner.

"Good," he said, relaxing. "I'm forever telling gay boys that they're gay before they realize it. It can get embarrassing."

It was at this point that my eyes popped out of my skull, landed on the floor, and rolled under the refrigerator. Figuratively speaking, of course.

I did close my eyes for a moment just to make sure they didn't go anywhere. It wasn't like this was some shocking revelation, but it was the first time it was being said out loud. At least, with me in the room.

"Seriously, I can't imagine why anyone wouldn't sing it from the mountaintop," he said—no, he *sang* from atop the couch. "But it's not my place to out anyone, so your secret's safe with me. I mean . . . it *is* a secret, right? Sam's never said anything."

"No," I said. "I mean, yes. I mean, no it's not a secret, but Sam and I have never talked about it. There's a lot that Sam and I don't talk about, apparently."

"I doubt that," he said, as he dropped down beside me on

the beanbag chair. "Come now, tell Mamma what's wrong."

"Well, at this precise moment, what's wrong is that this beanbag chair was definitely not built for two," I said, pushing myself up to my feet. "But, really, it's nothing. This is our last Saturday night before we both go back to school. It's not time for serious. Let's have fun."

"Huzzah!" Marq cheered as he bounced out of the beanbag chair and several feet into the air, nearly banging his head on the ceiling. Flouncing over to the closet, he reached in and withdrew what I initially believed to be some crazy tropical bird. I was only slightly relieved to watch him unfurl it into a pink feather boa that perfectly matched his nails. He threw the boa around his neck with a flourish (naturally) and said, "Exeunt!"

Actually, he kind of looked like the drama teacher in *High School Musical*. But not as masculine.

After a brief reflective pause when I wondered what I'd gotten myself into, I followed him out of the trailer. "Nice boa," I said.

"Accessories are the most important part of any outfit," he said, grabbing my arm and pulling me toward him. He is *very* grabby. "Speaking of . . . do you wear that fine fedora everywhere you go?"

"Almost."

"And people think *I'm* gay."

"You are."

"Honey, that's what I'm saying."

Suddenly my hat felt about a hundred pounds heavier on

my head and I was imagining it all lit up in bright colors . . . with its own pink feathers. Oddly, it never looked that way on my grandfather, who was the fedora's previous owner. I'd always thought he looked debonair in a thirties flashback kind of way. I'd *assumed* that it made me look the same.

Guess not.

Marq gushed on as we walked through the maze of trailers. The scent of pot was much stronger now. I took it to mean that the owners of that particular wheeled home were back in residence. It was also possible that the harlot's RV was rocking ever so slightly as we passed. I tried to ignore what could be going on inside that was powerful enough to make an RV rock, and quickened my step ever so slightly to get us out of there. People were obviously starting home from the faire and I wanted to escape the parking lot before the traffic got overwhelming.

And maybe part of me—a miniscule, slightly close-minded part of me—wanted to be clear before anyone saw me walking with a guy in a feather boa and pink nail polish. Even Ren Faire folk might find that bizarre. Whereas in West Hollywood, it was only slightly eccentric.

It took less time to work my way back through the maze of mobile homes now that I was with someone who knew where he was going without relying on landmarks. The whole way, Marq was going on about how he was excited about our night on the town. I think I managed a couple enthusiastic moans at the right pauses in conversation to give him the impression that I was listening. In truth, I was kind of lost in several thoughts at the same time. Between wondering what else Sam was withholding from me and questioning exactly how gay our gay old time was going to be in WeHo, my mind was fairly full. That is, until I was pulled back into the moment when his grip on my arm threatened to rip it out of the socket and his naturally high-pitched voice went into the realm of a whistling teakettle.

"Why, it's Greased Lightning!" he shrieked, bouncing up and down and taking my arm along with him.

"Actually," I said, trying to extricate myself from the vise that was his hand. "We call her Electra."

"Well, she's *electrifying*," he said. And I guess she was. Like my fedora, I'd inherited Electra from the same grandpa who used to take me to the Adamson Country Club, back before it was condemned and only suitable for hosting events where the peasantry would gather en masse. Electra is a 1957 Ford Fairlane Skyliner with a convertible hardtop that no longer converts. She's red and white with a silver lightning bolt of a stripe that splits the top from the bottom and serves as the inspiration for the car's name.

Back when I got Electra, I did consider naming her after the famed car from *Grease*, but it seemed kind of an obvious choice. And so, Electra was born . . . or reborn, really. I even had a naming ceremony where I bounced an empty plastic Cherry Coke bottle off her fender. This was before I knew Sam or was close to Hope, so it was a considerably lackluster ceremony what with just me and the car. It was also a couple years before I could drive, so one might say it was premature as well.

I went around to the driver's side, got in and started her up, all while Marq continued to stand outside. "You getting in?" I asked.

"A polite gentleman opens a door for a lady," Marq said, fluffing his feather boa.

My teeth automatically clenched. It's not like Marq was the first queen I'd ever met. My mom's best friend and business partner, Blaine, is friends with some of the nelliest queens this side of the audience for a Kathy Griffin show. However, I've never fully understood men who behave like they're women.

Not that there's anything wrong with that.

I chose not to respond, but raised my eyebrows in his direction. I guess he took my meaning because he got into Electra without any fanfare. "Fine," he said. "But I refuse to accompany you to the submarine races."

I vaguely understood the fifties reference, but shook it from my mind before it took hold there and caused me any real concern. While I started Electra and listened for the signs that told me she was going to be a good girl and drive, Marq picked up my portable iPod radio from the seat between us. Since Electra only gets AM—and only when she's in the mood—her optional stereo system can be removed from her at a moment's notice. It was a new option that I'd added after getting stuck behind an accident on the PCH for an hour over the summer. I was only four blocks from my house, but trapped with no alternate routes. I'd even considered abandoning Electra after sixty minutes condemned to the traffic with nothing but my own thoughts to keep me company.

Sometimes my own thoughts would be enough to drive anyone insane.

"Seeing how we're two gay boys about to hit WeHo," Marq said. It was like he needed to keep reminding me I was gay. As if it was something I was going to forget any time soon. "I'm thinking we need some Cher! To get us in the mood."

"Um . . . ," I said, worrying what *mood* he was going for. "I don't have any Cher."

"Okay, then," he cheered on. "Madge!"

"I'm sorry?"

"Ma*donna*!"

"Oh," I said. "Uh . . ."

"No Madonna! And you call yourself gay!"

"Not that often."

"Well, who *do* you have from the milieu of gay party boy musical stylings? Gwen? Fergie?"

"Yes!" I said with more enthusiasm than it really warranted. Either Marq's exuberance was catching, or I felt like I had to overcompensate in defense of my gayness. For some reason, I felt like pointing out that I also had some vintage Kylie Minogue on there as if that would impress him or something. I managed to subdue that impulse as he turned up the Fergie and we drove along in Electra, alternating between stomping our feet and spelling out words as we sang along to the music.

All in all, it wasn't a horrible start to the evening.

Until his hand latched on to mine.

And would not let go.

On the Town

Marq thought we were on a date.

What was initially pitched as a group function was whittled down to a trio, then ditched down to a duo that Marq now thought had the potential for a coupling. At least, that's what his tight clutch on my hand was telling me. I wasn't entirely sure how I felt about that. Or how to respond. I'd never been on a date before, unless you count going to the prom with Suze. Which I didn't. To get all dressed up, pick up a guy, and take him out . . . that was a new experience for me. One that I wasn't sure I was ready for or even wanted to be ready for in this case.

It wasn't like Marq was some loser I'd be disgusted over the mere idea of going out with. He was kind of cute in a dorky way. He was kind of fun in a slightly overwhelming way. He was kind of a lot of things in a lot of ways, but each one came with a disclaimer that made him not really my type.

Not that I knew what my type really was. I had an idea of the guy I'd like to date. A pretty good idea, too. And, while Marq didn't exactly fit that picture, he got points for the one quality no other guy possessed.

He seemed to be interested in me.

That was a new one. At least, so far as I knew.

Too bad his interest lasted right up until he was distracted by the shiny lights of West Hollywood.

"O-M-G!" Marq exclaimed as we reached the gay part of Santa Monica Boulevard. And may I add how much I *love* (heavy sarcasm) people who speak in text message terms without irony. That was another check in the "against" column on the concept of Marq as date potential. "It's like I've come home!" Then, he opened the window and yelled out "WeHo! Take me, I'm yours!"

On the bright side, he released my hand.

On the dark side, several people yelled things back that are *so* not printable here. Not because they were mean. Because they were very, *very* dirty.

I stopped and started my way through traffic—something Electra really doesn't like to do—as I sought out a side street to park on. When that turned out to be a pointless exercise, I finally settled on paid parking at the Pacific Design Center since it was only a couple bucks and didn't require me to parallel park. Parallel parking was also not a plus for my big baby, Electra.

While I was paying the lot entrance fee, my cell phone starting vibrating on the seat next to me. Before I could maneuver the money out the window to the attendant and twist to get the phone, Marq had it in his hands and was pushing some buttons. Mostly mine.

"Don't forget me," he read. "Who is this Suze and why's she afraid you're going to forget her?"

I completed the transaction and pulled into the lot, biting back a lecture on touching other people's property. "She's the friend that keeps getting me locked in the stocks."

"Pillory," he corrected.

"Pillory," I replied as he pushed even more buttons. "What are you doing now?"

"Nothing," he said in the least innocent voice I think I'd ever heard in my entire life.

I snatched my phone back from him and checked the display. He'd already sent a reply. It read, "I could never forget you."

I seethed in my seat.

Obviously, Suze was referring to me picking her up at the airport, but there was something about Marq's reply that left things open to interpretation. Then again, I probably would have written the same thing back, just as innocently, so I tried not to be too annoyed. To avoid any further unwanted texts, I slipped the phone into my front pocket so it was less accessible.

It was still somewhat early for a Saturday night, but Santa Monica Boulevard was already littered with pretty boys only slightly older than us . . . or made up to look like they were only slightly older than us. All of them were dressed in tight T-shirts and even tighter jeans. I was glad that Hope and Sam weren't with us, so I could have the freedom to openly gawk. Then I wondered why I felt like I couldn't openly gawk with my friends along.

We stopped to take in our surroundings. There was so much to do, but so many restrictions. We were too young to hit the clubs. The one bookstore that wasn't "adults only" was packed for a book signing. And the nearest coffeehouse seemed to be having their own lesbian poetry night, because one look at the patrons suggested that we'd kind of stand out. I guess I wasn't the only one who noticed because Marq turned to me, adopted a southern tone and said, "Oh, Rhett, where will we go? What will we do?"

"Food," I said, largely because it was the only suggestion I could come up with . . . and I was starving. "There's a pizza place over there." I pointed across the street, down about a block from where we were. Blaine had taken me there many times growing up. According to him, it was one of the few places in Los Angeles you could get a good slice. I figured with a world weary traveler like Marq with me, I couldn't suggest any old pizza joint. Of course, by "pizza joint" I meant a trendy, yet elegant, sidewalk cafe with candlelight, soft music playing, and faux marble finish on the walls. I briefly worried that he might get the wrong idea, but since he already seemed to be working the whole wrong idea, what harm could it do?

When the bouncing started again, I took it to mean that Marq liked the plan. No wonder he was so thin. He was constantly working off calories with his exuberance.

We bypassed the outside tables and headed into the restaurant. The street was getting busy with Labor Day weekend tourists, and I was already over the whole crowd thing after two days at the faire. We lucked out when a circular booth opened up in the front corner right after we stepped inside. The hostess took us directly to the seats, tugging on Marq's boa to lead us all the way.

As it turned out the circular booth wasn't all that lucky. Marq took the opportunity to slide all the way in and sit several inches into my personal space. His hand was practically vibrating and I could only suspect he was debating whether or not to grab mine again.

The waiter came right up, saving us from small talk and awkward hand maneuvering. Seeing as how we were both in the mood for pizza, we didn't bother looking at the menu. We each ordered a soda, had a brief debate over the virtues of mushrooms (him) and black olives (me) as the toppings, decided on getting our own slices rather than a whole pie, then sent the waiter on his merry way.

At which point, the awkward silence ensued.

We'd been doing so well while in motion. Singing along to the radio. Checking out the eye candy on the street. But now that we were stationary in a romantic dinner spot, I guess we were both feeling overwhelmed by the implications. This is something that happens a lot with me in life. I can't imagine it was a familiar feeling for Marq. He tends to be the type to overwhelm, not the other way around.

Naturally, he was the one to break the silence.

"Sam tells me you have this hyphen system where you put people in nice little boxes according to who you think they are. What's that about?"

The waiter raised an eyebrow in my direction as he dropped off our sodas. When Marq put it like that, it made me sound a bit like an ass. I could read the look on the waiter's face, seeing me as some spoiled L.A. brat who thought he was superior to everyone. That is *so* not me.

The "spoiled L.A." part, I mean. I fully cop to the feelings of superiority. I mean, have you *met* some of the people I go to school with?

That's a joke. I only *wish* I felt superior. The opposite is usually true.

"I don't put them in boxes," I said, more to the waiter than to Marq. "And it's not *my* system. It's the way everyone in this town operates. The more hyphens you have between your job titles, the more important you are. You know, actor-director-producer. That kind of thing. I just take that and apply it to my friends."

"Do me!" he exclaimed.

I choked on my Sprite. "Excuse me?"

"Do my hyphens!" he explained. "What box would you put me in?"

Oh, the options for that answer were endless.

"I don't know all that much about you," I said, even though I kind of did. More than I wanted to, in fact. Like he had a feather fetish and a penchant for wearing dresses. "How would you describe yourself?"

Marq stopped buzzing long enough to think about it. "Well, first and foremost, I am Gay." Then there was a pause where I think he was expecting me to make a joke or something, which only made the stony silence that followed more uncomfortable.

"That's not quite the point," I finally said. "It's more the things that you do, not the things that you are. Like, when I come up with the hyphenate, I wouldn't say you're a boy. Or that you're Latino. It's more the things you have control over. Your choices."

"But I choose to be Gay," he repeated. "Capital G, Gay. Whereas you are little *g*, gay . . . very little *g*, actually." I wasn't sure if that was an insult, but I was taking it as one. "Therefore," he continued, "I consider myself, first and foremost: Gay."

"Fine," I said. We were working on *his* hyphenate. If he wanted to do it wrong, that was his problem. "You're Gay. Marq with a *q* is Gay with a capital G. So that makes you a Gay-Ren Faire Performing-drag quee—"

"I'm not a drag queen," he said. Not defensively, but definitively.

"But—"

"Dressing as the queen is occupational," he explained. "Not recreational. To be a drag queen is a lifestyle choice. A calling. One I'm not sure I'm ready to answer to beyond the Ren Faire . . . and the occasional Halloween . . . and maybe the homecoming court elections, depending on the fabulousness of my new school. But full-time? I'm not quite there yet."

"Duly noted. So, what else do you do? Do you sing? Do you dance?"

He nodded. "And I look mighty fine in a tight pair of pants. As I'm sure you've already noticed."

I took a long sip from my soda, draining it to nearly empty while my eyes remained focused on the ice cubes in front of me.

"I take that as a no comment," he added, with a flirtatious brush of his hand against my not-quite-as-tight pants. "On the subject of body-hugging garments . . ." He raised his eyebrows a couple times, tilting his head toward the door where a trio of guys had come in wearing pants so tight I worried they were cutting off their circulation to their toes.

They had to be in their mid-twenties. Spent most of their day at the gym. Either independently wealthy or somebodies in the film industry to be able to afford the clothes they were wearing. Then again, the outfits may have been from a secondhand shop. Clearly, they hadn't been able to find anything in their true sizes.

Not that I was complaining.

We both lost track of the conversation as we gaped openly at them until one of them caught me staring. My eyes shot down to the table, where I was surprised to find our food had been delivered and my drink refilled while I was lost in thought. When I checked back to see if Marq had noticed the arrival of our dinner, I was surprised to see that he was locked in a staring contest with not one, but two of the three guys. Which is quite impressive when you think about it, since his two eyes were locked with four.

"Marq," I said, with a slight jab to his ribs. What? Like he hadn't been manhandling me for the past two days.

Wait. That doesn't sound right.

"Oh, come on," he said, pulling his attention back to me. "It doesn't hurt to look. Well, okay, maybe it aches a smidge. But it's a good kind of ache."

I knew exactly what he meant.

When I stole a glance back at the trio, they were heading to a table on the other side of the room. The one nearest me threw a wink in my direction, and I didn't even blush with embarrassment.

With Marq, I was feeling more Capital G Gay than I'd ever felt before in my life. Probably had something to do with him having more than enough Gay to overflow into everyone else in the vicinity. It wasn't like I'd ever actively tried to hide this side of me, but I'd never been so open with it before.

And I'm not talking about how I randomly break out into show tunes, either.

"Where were we?" I asked, focusing back on our conversation.

"You mean before we got lost in their pants?" Marq asked. "We were finding my hyphenate."

"Right," I said. "You're a Gay-Ren Faire performing-singer-dancer-actor. A quadruple hyphenate. Quite impressive." But in my mind I downgraded him to a triple, since I honestly don't consider "gay" to be a hyphen-worthy descriptor whether you spell it "gay," "Gay," or "GAY!!" (That last one should be sung in a high octave to give the proper effect.) This has nothing to do with me not even being able to figure out my own hyphenate. Totally unrelated.

We fell into silence as we started on our slices. I'd opted for no olives and went with a plain slice while he'd ordered the— I kid you not—Rainbow Special, which was a pizza so over-loaded with colorful veggies that it looked like he had his own triangular gay pride flag on his plate.

While I was busy enjoying both my pizza and a silence that I didn't find nearly as awkward as the last, Marq burst out with, "What was the worst day of your life?"

Again, I choked on my Sprite. "Excuse me?!"

"That's a game *I* play," he said. "It's a good conversation starter when the conversation lulls."

I preferred the lull.

"Still, you could . . . you know . . . lead up to it or something," I said, clearing my throat. I guess lulls in conversation are unusual for Marq. What with how he's always buzzing about something. "Tell me yours first."

"That'd be the day the baseball team beat the crap out of me for wearing this very same feather boa to gym class." He lifted his floppy black hair to show me a small scar. "Five stitches." Marq said this all with his usual amount of bubbly personality. There wasn't a trace of reverence for the horrific situation he was describing. I almost, for a second, thought that maybe he was making it up. But what kind of person would make up that kind of story and then tell it with such lighthearted aplomb?

Then, I saw something in his eyes; a depth of sorrow I'd never noticed before. Behind all the bluster he was just another scared kid. Like me. Only his fears were, apparently, real. Which just made me feel all the more idiotic about not finding a way to out myself, without making a production of outing myself, yet.

"That was about when my parents thought I should be home schooled," he explained, still all lightness and mirth. "And we started the Ren Faire circuit year-round. Your turn!"

Blink. Blink.

I wanted to ask him more about his experience. I wanted to talk about my own fears. Not that I thought the Orion baseball team would react the same way. Particularly since we don't have a baseball team. But, the guys on the soccer team would be more likely to defend me than to take me on. Not that I would be wearing any feather boas to school. But, some might think of my fedora as a different kind of feather boa. Marq had already commented on the fedora's gay quotient.

Was I just as out of the closet as Marq without even realizing it? Were we more alike than I wanted to admit?

With all those questions zipping around my brain, I blurted out the only answer that didn't require me to think, "The day of my grandfather's funeral." In hindsight, even if I had thought about it, that would have been my answer. It was the one day that haunts me in my dreams and surprises me with teary eyes at the most unexpected times.

There was a pause while he absorbed my answer. "Wow. That totally sucks!"

"I know," I said, softly and with more reverence than he had used when sharing his own personal tragedy.

"No," he said. "I mean it sucks that that's the worst tragedy you've ever had!"

Blink. Blink. Blink.

"Well," he backtracked, "it's not like . . . I mean . . . it's sad and all, but I was hoping for something more original. Something truly tragic. I mean, all my grandparents have died and it was, you know, *upsetting*. But that's what grandparents do. They die. Eventually, I mean."

"Oh, and your beating by the baseball team wasn't a big ol' cliché?" I spouted out before I realized just what I was saying. But, rather than be all shocked at me, Marq simply laughed. Either he was incredibly well-adjusted or totally messed up.

Probably both.

"If that was the worst day you've ever had," Marq added, "then I'd say you've lived a wonderful life. Boring. But not that bad."

I bit into my pizza and let his comment hang in the air. I had no intention of explaining any further or trying to defend the depths of despair I have experienced in my clearly overprotected world. My story may lack the drama of a gay bashing, but it was a pivotal moment in my life, all the same. Besides, if he really wanted to seriously examine it, he would have asked why I was talking about the day of the funeral and not the actual day my grandfather died.

But I wasn't about to get into that with him.

Prelude to a Kiss

"Don't get all sullen on me now," Marq said between sips of soda. "The debauchery hasn't even started yet. At least wait until we've been turned away from a couple bars."

"Well, don't be all judging my sad past," I said, with semi-faux pout.

"You are absolutely right. That was horrifically hetero of me. We gays are supposed to be sensitive and turn to one another for comfort and fashion tips. Barkeep, another Sprite for my friend here!"

The waiter—and several patrons—glared in our direction. This was so not the type of place you yelled out orders. Though the trio of tight pants seemed to appreciate Marq's enthusiasm. And Marq appreciated their appreciation.

As the waiter brought me my third soda of the evening, Marq started bouncing again. "I went online earlier and found a club down the street that's having an eighteen and over night!"

"But you're not eighteen," I reminded him. "And I don't even turn seventeen until the end of the month."

"Oh, you really are just a babe," he replied. "Like they're going to turn us away. Sixteen. Eighteen. What's the difference? We're young. We're cute. They'll stamp our hands so we can't drink and let us go. Trust me. I've gotten away with this all over the world."

I considered all the ways his plan was doomed to failure, but kept my mouth shut. He'd figure it out once we got turned away at the door. WeHo takes its underage partying very seriously. Unless you're a celebrity. Then it's carte blanche, even if you're twelve.

We finished our slices, fought over who paid, and left a generous tip because I was pretty sure Marq had annoyed our waiter when he joked that his Rainbow Special didn't feel like it had enough pride because the kitchen skimped on the green peppers.

"This way," Marq directed as we left the restaurant. Being that it was his little Pride Parade, I followed dutifully.

Santa Monica Boulevard was heating up. Throngs of men were walking up and down the street between the clubs and restaurants. We did our fair share of gawking as, I'm pleased to say, we were gawked at a couple of times ourselves.

"Don't look now," Marq said. "But look behind us."

I didn't even try to figure that one out as I threw a glance over my shoulder. The three guys from the restaurant were walking in our wake. I couldn't tell if they were following us or if they were just heading in the same direction. Either way, I wasn't about to go down any dark alleys.

Paul Ruditis

I turned back to Marq. "You don't think—"

"That they're hot for our bods?" he asked with a giggle. "Can you blame them?"

In that moment, I felt both incredibly tense and incredibly comfortable at the same time. I guess Marq noticed because he chose that moment to reopen our earlier discussion. "So, why haven't you told Sam?"

"Told Sam what?" I asked.

"Told Sam that you like the company of boys," Marq clarified, throwing a look over his shoulder.

I knew we weren't going to get through the night without having this conversation. I decided to head it off with my usual, "Sam's never told me that she's straight."

Marq rolled his eyes at me. "That's different."

"No," I said. "Actually, it isn't. Just because we're gay doesn't mean we have to be Gay. It's your choice to live as a Capital G. I'm fine with my little *g*."

Marq shot me a sly smile.

"That's not what I meant!"

"Just because you're out doesn't mean you have to be flamboyant," Marq said. "And what's wrong with being flamboyant, anyway?"

Great. Now I'd gone and offended him.

"It's not about flamboyance," I clarified. "It's about who I am. Once I'm out, I'm going to be the 'gay kid.' No matter what I do. I'm not big on labels. I just want to be Bryan."

He gave me a hard look. "Whether or not you're out," he said, "you're still going to be labeled. That's high school.

That's life." Before I could think of something to say, Marq started bouncing again, indicating that the conversation was closed for the time being. "Listen," he said, "can't you hear the *thumpa thumpa?*"

Oh, dear. Of course, I could hear it. Half the block could hear it. The DJ had the music blaring through the walls of the club. But the *thumpa thumpa* that was thumping the loudest wasn't the music. It was my heartbeat. I finally saw where he was taking me.

"Embers?" I asked as we reached the line for the club with the literally flaming theme. Seriously. Giant torches with fire shooting ten feet into the air sat on either side of the entrance. Red lights strobed on the rooftop. Bursts of hot air blew out the door and onto the street. It was like we were about to enter Hell . . . in so many ways.

"We can't get into Embers," I said as Marq forced me to the end of the line.

"Why not?"

I rose up on tiptoe and strained to see over the crowd, confirming my worst fears. "I know the bouncer," I said. A big, muscular guy I'd been acquainted with for many, many years was seated on a stool checking IDs at the front of the line. It was Blaine's ex-boyfriend. That's right. The ex of my mom's oldest and dearest friend was guarding the door to my first gay club. We're not talking one of those brief flings where there wasn't much chance of me being recognized. For a time, I'd called him Uncle Lonnie. There was no way we were getting into the club now. Even worse. There was no way this wasn't getting back to Blaine. He and Uncle Lonnie had parted on good terms and kept in touch.

"Excellent," Marq said. "There's no way he'd turn you away. Sneaking into a club is an integral experience in a gay boy's development. Everyone knows that."

Marq did not seem to understand the severity of the situation. Lonnie would *tell* Blaine.

As we shuffled closer to the door, I noticed the guys from the restaurant had lined up a few people behind us. Great. Now, not only was I going to be embarrassed in front of a bunch of total strangers, but also a trio of total strangers who seemed interested in me. Not that I had any plans to do anything with older guys. But I can imagine, can't I?

"This is *so* not going to work," I said as we got closer to the door.

"Not if you have that attitude, Gloomy Gus," Marq said, throwing an arm around me and giving a squeeze. "Just follow me."

As we reached the door, I hid myself behind Marq, figuring it was possible that Lonnie would turn him away without even seeing me. It was dark out, after all . . . so long as you ignored the massive amount of light the torches were throwing off.

"Bryan?" Lonnie said. "Why are you hiding behind that boy?"

So much for that.

I peeked out over Marq's shoulder. "Hi," I said. "We were just . . ."

"Wondering what the crowd was like tonight," Marq quickly jumped in. "We were just at Rage and it was totally dead."

"Somehow, I doubt either of you got into Rage," Lonnie said.

"Okay," Marq said. "Busted. We're not twenty-one."

Lonnie shook his head, looking right at me. "Does he think he's fooling anyone?"

"Only himself," I said, leaning in. "Look, it's my friend's only weekend in L.A. and he really wanted to come here. I told him we couldn't get in, but he's kind of delusional. All I ask is . . . could you just not embarrass us when you turn us away?"

Lonnie smiled at me in a friendly, not even remotely condescending way, and I wondered why he and Blaine ever broke up. Uncle Lonnie had always been a good guy. He proved himself to be an even better guy when he took my hand and stamped it with a red flame. "If I see you with an alcoholic beverage in your hand, I will have Blaine here in thirty seconds."

I tried to ignore Marq, who was excitedly beating on my shoulder. "So, Blaine's not inside?" I asked, hopefully.

"He's down the street. At Rage," Lonnie said. "I saw him earlier."

Great. Blaine was in WeHo too. Not much of a surprise considering he lived there, but I'd been deluding myself into believing he was probably out on the town elsewhere. Now, I had to hope that Rage wasn't totally dead like Marq had lied about it being. The last thing I needed was him popping up at Embers.

After Lonnie stamped Marq's hand, the two of us entered through the heat-blast opening. We paid the cover charge inside and made our way to the dance floor.

The fire theme was even more overwhelming on the inside. Flames shot across the ceiling while red and orange light filled the huge room. Naturally, there were fireplaces in every corner with softly glowing, burning embers that pulsed rather erotically. It was an interesting special effect.

Vents blew cool air onto the dance floor to compensate for the fire and dancing body heat. With the warm and cold fronts fighting for dominance, I was kind of surprised that there wasn't a thunderstorm forming over the dance floor. All in all, it was the dumbest design for a place I'd ever seen in my life.

It was *awesome*.

"I can't believe we're in!" Marq yelled over the music, which was funny considering how sure he'd been earlier.

"It helps to have connections in this town," I hollered back, like it wasn't pure luck that we'd gotten inside.

We'd gotten *inside*.

Sure, I'd been to WeHo many times before. I'd been out with the gays on Halloween. I'd even been to a couple pride parades. Seeing men dancing around in various states of undress wasn't entirely unusual. But, at the same time, it was.

I was at my first club. My first gay club.

"Let's dance!" Marq screamed as he pulled me onto the dance floor.

The music had switched to Xtina. One of her songs that I didn't know. But it didn't matter. I didn't hear the music so much as felt it. In a sea of gay men—and a few of the women who love them—I never felt more in tune with *everything*.

The dance floor was packed, but I didn't care. Not even when we were fighting for space up against a column in the middle of the floor. I just let myself go. I stopped worrying about Sam's issues. About my issues. About everything.

And I *danced*.

As I moved to the music, I noticed the three guys from the restaurant on the edge of the dance floor looking in our direction. I was going to tell Marq to check out the guys checking us out when the look in his eyes stopped me dead in my tracks. I'd been to enough movies in my life to know what that expression meant.

Before I could do anything, Marq was leaning even more into my personal space. His eyes were closed and his lips were puckered. As those lips started to brush against mine, I reflexively pulled away with such a surprising amount of force that I slammed the back of my skull into the wooden column so hard that I saws stars.

And not the kind of stars the paparazzi were stalking on the streets of Hollywood.

Last of the Red Hot Lovers

My head was hurting Sunday morning. I was pretty sure it was a phantom pain, like when someone loses an arm or a leg but still feels it like it was never gone. I'd lost all respect for myself and my brain kept insisting that I hadn't really done anything wrong. It wasn't like I'd planned to pull away from Marq's kiss so violently. It was just a reflex action. Which, I guess, only made it worse.

Marq had played things off pretty well following the aborted kiss. He just kept dancing as if nothing had happened. Me? I was too busy trying to come up with an apology that wouldn't sound all pathetic and/or insulting. By the time the song changed, I figured it was too late to say anything, so I fell into the rhythm and continued to dance the night away. The trio from the restaurant never did wind up approaching us.

"What are you, antiquing the counter?" Blaine asked,

pulling me out of my memory. "Stop that before you wipe off all the paint."

I rolled my eyes like he was talking crazy, but I guess I was the one with the mental deficiency. I'd been wiping down the same spot for something like the past five minutes. The paint really wasn't in jeopardy, but that part of the counter was as clean as it was going to get.

We were in my mom's new store, Kaye 9: Li'l Beaches. Like her original shop in Malibu—the original Kaye 9—the store featured her dogwear designs along with high-end accessories and toys for people with a love for their canines . . . and a fair amount of disposable income. The new location was the reason our family vacation had been pushed up a month and culled down to one week. Mom would have canceled entirely since we went away the week before the store opened, but Blaine had insisted we go away as much for her sanity as his own. While we were gone, he was able to put the finishing touches on the store and even plan the opening night party where, I admit, I partook in a fair amount of champagne.

With two stores, Kaye 9 was now a chain. We'd doubled the staff. I was second assistant manager of Li'l Beaches. Sam was hired as a part-time employee, though she got the weekend off for the Ren Faire. I offered Hope a job also, but she claims to eschew work for more artistic pursuits. To be honest, if my dad was litigator to the stars, I'd eschew work too. As it is, I don't quite understand what my dad does or why it takes him to all corners of the globe, but my friends and I have a lot of fun trying to figure it out. Lately, we've been thinking that he trains rebel fighters in third world countries. I even tried to search his stuff for clues to this while we were vacationing in Vancouver, but he pulled his usual act and left all his work behind so he could focus on me and Mom.

Damn him for his family values.

"We've got a few minutes before the store opens," Blaine said. "If you want to talk about why you're massaging the counter more thoroughly than my last boyfriend, the aromatherapy masseur, ever massaged anything."

The masseur had come long after Lonnie, but the mention of exes only brought my mind back to my embarrassment. Blaine hadn't given me any indication that Lonnie had said anything about my club hopping. Or, really, my club *hop*. That could either mean that Lonnie hadn't told him, or that Blaine was holding the information for some future time. Until then, it was easier for me to focus on the aromatherapy masseur.

"Is that even a real job?" I asked.

"Licensed and everything. Not everybody can be a canine design entrepreneur, you know," Blaine said, reminding me that in Los Angeles, anything could be a job. And usually was. "So, what's the deal?"

"Just the end of summer blahs," I lied. It was so much more complicated than that. Blaine was the perfect person to talk about it with, but I couldn't manage to work up the . . . nerve? . . . interest? . . . intestinal fortitude? (That last one means I was getting sick to my stomach.)

"Well, the Back-to-School Picnic seems the perfect cure for that," Blaine said, though the smirk on his face assured me that he hadn't gone totally bonkers. Like any school function was going to be the solution to *any* problem. Particularly one where people might be expecting me to get onstage and perform. Alongside the guy who tried to kiss me. And the friends who didn't know.

"You know where I am if you change your mind and want to talk," Blaine added. "Over there, restocking the doggie doo shovels."

"We go through a lot of those out here," Mom noted as she joined us. We all smiled at the humor implicit in that statement, then broke to continue prepping the store for opening. Well, they continued, I went back to my daydreaming. Or, daynightmaring is more like it.

Would my friends know about what happened between me and Marq? Or what didn't happen? Sure, Marq had said he wouldn't tell anyone about my closeted status, but that was before I spurned his advances, as they say in old movies. What if he tried to exact some revenge to make him feel better? What if he decided to hold it over my head? What if I got back to work and stopped all this worrying?

Taking the easiest chore I could find, I started organizing the dog collars into their proper sections—leather studded collars up high, and fluffy bejeweled ones down low—where the kids could get to them and force their parents to buy them.

Outside the front window, the overly tanned Malibu wives with their overly tanned children and their overly tanned dogs were already waiting to come in. It was about ten minutes from opening, but when I saw both Mom and Blaine eyeing the crowd, I figured we'd probably unlock the doors early. A fight was looking about to brew between a pit bull and a Chihuahua. I know that might seem unbalanced, but that little Chihuahua is one of our meanest customers. She can totally hold her own.

While we were looking out the window deciding whether or not to open early, Blaine drew my attention to a totally different matter. "What is that?" he asked.

I looked past the pooches to the parking lot where I saw Hope squeezing out of a tiny pink and purple car dressed in full-on Renaissance Faire attire. She was alone. No Sam.

No surprise.

"You know. The Ren Faire is in town," I reminded him, since he was the one who had given Sam off for the event.

"That's right," he replied. "And here I left my tights at home."

Hope's purple cape cut a swath through the crowd to the front door. She didn't bother knocking to let us know she was there. I guess she figured there was no way we could miss her.

"Might as well open up," Mom said as she went to the door and unlocked it. "Milady," she added as Hope slipped in first.

"Thanks, Kaye," she replied, then exchanged hellos with Blaine.

Mom threw the door all the way open and greeted her adoring public. By the time everyone was inside, she was covered in dog slobber and somehow managed to get a lollipop stuck to her cheek.

What's that saying about never working with children or animals?

Yuck.

"You sure you don't want to come to the faire?" Hope asked when she got to me. I'd begged off via text message earlier, not wanting to deal with Marq first thing in the morning. "Did something happen with you and Marq last night?" she asked, getting all scary psychic again.

"What? Marq? No!"

Smooth, Bryan.

Somehow, Blaine was suddenly behind me. "Mark?" he asked. "Who's Mark?" (*Aside:* I'm spelling it like that here because there isn't a chance in the world that Blaine would have ever guessed that his name had a "q" in it.)

"Sam's gay best friend," Hope said.

"And when did we start putting people in categories?" Blaine asked.

Pretty much always, I thought. But I didn't say that. "Oh, no, it's okay," I said. "Marq's like über-gay. He likes to be known as Sam's gay best friend."

"And what, exactly, does one have to do to be über-gay?" Blaine asked. "I assume you don't mean he's been sleeping with a whole lot of guys because that's not safe behavior."

"You know," I said, remembering the story he'd told me on the drive home. "He came out to his parents back when he was six. After he redesigned the wardrobes for all Sam's Barbies. He told everyone he wanted to be a gay fashion designer when he grew up."

"No," Blaine said, with a light voice that betrayed the slightest hint of an edge. "That's when he first knew he was a stereotype. Mark knew that he was gay the first time he was attracted to another boy."

"It's Marq, actually," I said, just to be arbitrary. "With a *q*."

Blaine didn't even bat an eye. He's used to my arbitrariness.

"What about you, Blaine?" Hope asked. "How did you come out?

"Badly," Blaine said.

I was so shocked over his response that I took a step back. I'd met Blaine's mamma several times. She didn't seem the type to have a bad reaction to the news. And he grew up in Pasadena, which was fairly liberal about these kinds of things. "How badly?" I asked, thinking back to Marq's tale of the baseball team.

"No," he said, "Not that kind of badly. The other kind."

There are two kinds of badly? I wondered. "Explain."

"The only thing missing from my coming out was a parade," he said.

Hope and I looked at each other. "Still not getting it," she said.

"It was senior year of high school," he said. "And I wanted to ask Tommy Gantz to the prom."

"You never told me about that," Mom said. I knew from stories and pictures that Blaine and Mom wound up going to the prom together. As friends, naturally.

"Once he got Jenn Torres pregnant it seemed pointless," Blaine said. "Didn't realize it *wasn't* pointless until we hooked up later at your Fourth of July pool party, but that's a different story. A *very* different story." One that I didn't want to hear. Listening to Blaine talk about past conquests was like hearing my parents talk about sex. Icky.

"Anyway," I said, waving my hand to get him moving along.

"Anyway," he replied. "I thought if I was going to ask a guy out, then I should make things formal first. So, of course, I came out to your mom. She was totally cool about it."

"As you knew she would be," Mom said.

"As I knew she would be," Blaine repeated. "Then I told my mom."

"Who was also very cool with it," Mom said, with a laugh.

Hope and I looked to Blaine for an explanation. "She threw me a party."

We burst out laughing. "A coming-out party?" I asked.

"Yes, smart-ass," Blaine said. "She threw me a coming-out party. Complete with rainbow decorations and a Liza Minnelli impersonator. It was humiliating. She invited half the school and every gay person she'd ever met."

"It wasn't that bad," Mom said. "It was the social event of the year. Everyone was talking about it."

"Exactly," Blaine said. "*Everyone.* I suddenly became the poster child for the well-adjusted gay teen. The prom committee wanted me to head up decorations. Girls were asking my advice for what they should wear. Straight guys that I had no interest in whatsoever were suddenly trying to get me to do things for them that their girlfriends wouldn't. I was the most popular kid in school because I was the first one to formally come out. Everyone wanted a piece of me. All but Tommy, that is. He wouldn't even come near me."

"Not for a few months, at least," I added.

Blaine smacked me on the shoulder. "This is my tragic tale," he said. "Let me tell it my way."

"Sorry," I said, hanging my head. I was trying to make light of the situation because he was describing my nightmare. I didn't want to be "the gay kid." I didn't want to lead off my hyphenate with a Capital G. Or even a little *g*. I just wanted to be Bryan. A normal, well-adjusted guy who blended into the background and just happened to like boys. Is that so wrong?

"Things eventually calmed down when everyone realized I was not about to be their performing monkey," Blaine said. "But the run up to prom was some of the most embarrassing weeks of my life."

"Except for all the action you were getting from the straight guys who you *were* interested in," Mom added.

Blaine shook his head. "I wonder why I even bother." He then looked to Hope. "Any reason you're asking?" I couldn't help but wonder a little myself.

"Nothing much," Hope said. "Drea kissed me last night and it got me thinking about the whole spectrum of sexuality."

"WHAT?!" I yelled, scaring every dog and child in the place. That was a stunning development to be dropped on us on a Sunday morning. I immediately pulled Hope into the back room so we could have some real privacy.

Those Malibu wives can be a gossipy bunch.

The Tap Dance Kid

Once we were alone in the backroom there was a moment of silent hesitation before I blurted out, "What do you mean, Drea kissed you?"

"Did I stutter?" Hope asked, getting surprisingly defensive. "Drea. Kissed. Me. On the lips. After the lesbian poetry night thing."

"And you spent the rest of the night tossing and turning, wondering what it all meant?" I said, revealing more than I'd intended about my own sleepless night after my own near same-sex kiss. "'Cause you look kind of tired."

"*Noooo*," she said. Like it was my fault for noticing her eyes were all droopy and the purple contacts she was wearing didn't have their usual glimmer. "I stayed up writing."

"Oh," I said. She was just tossing and turning things over in her mind, not in her bed. I didn't bother to point out how it was the same thing. "So, what does this kiss mean?"

"Why does it have to mean anything?" she asked, fiddling with one of the stuffed dogs we used in the store to model my mom's clothing. "It was a kiss. It was nice. It was over."

"Are you going to kiss her again?" I asked, when what I really wanted to know was if she was planning on doing anything else. Were she and Drea going to start dating? Were we going to be throwing a coming-out party for Hope?

"We'll see," Hope said cryptically. "And you don't have to worry about keeping anything from Sam. I told her earlier."

"I'm not the one keeping secrets." Okay. It was a lie. But Hope didn't know that. Except for the look on her face that suggested maybe she did. But, instead of saying anything about it, she simply walked back out to the front, making it clear that the subject was dropped.

For so many reasons, I felt like I'd just been hit by a semi-truck. And none of them had to do with my thoughts on Hope and Drea in the least. Hope had totally stolen my thunder. Now there was no way we could both come out without it becoming a huge deal in our small school community.

I followed Hope back out front where the action had slowed dramatically in the brief time we'd been in back. Only one woman and her beagle were in the store. They were looking at our Snoopy dog products, which was fitting, considering.

"Chase everyone away?" I asked Mom and Blaine.

"Most of them just came in for some Puppier Water for their morning strolls," Mom said, explaining the early morning sales. No surprise there. The high-priced, sparkling dog water was one of our top sellers now that we were near a beach that allowed dogs.

A bit of standing around ensued while we all looked for a safe subject for discussion. Hope was the first to come up with one, though I wasn't so sure that it met the "safe" qualification. "What did you and Marq do last night?" she asked innocently.

Stopped short of what you and Drea did, I thought. But what I said was, "Hung out. Nothing major. Had pizza." Everyone nodded like I lived an incredibly boring life. Which was just fine with me. Blaine's lack of reaction confirmed that Lonnie hadn't said anything. Yet.

"Well, I just stopped by to see if you changed your mind about the faire," Hope said. "You sure you don't want to join us?"

"Love to," I lied, grabbing the inventory book off the counter to make it look like I had some official assignment that simply needed to get done on a Sunday morning. Of Labor Day weekend. "Can't. We're swamped." All four of us looked to the lone patron in the store, who looked back at us in fear. Even she didn't buy it that our service was *that* attentive. "Besides," I added with my best fake pout. "I promised I'd pick up Suze at the airport."

"You're not fooling anyone with that fake pout," Hope said. Okay, so I guess my best wasn't good enough. I still had to pick up Suze, so it really didn't matter how convincing a show I put on about my feelings for missing the faire.

"You are coming by later to work on the skit, right?" she asked. "Five o'clock. I confirmed the time with Sam this morning."

"Wouldn't miss it," I said. In truth, it was more like "couldn't" miss it, because if I did, she and Sam would take turns beating the crap out of me. Not that I had to say that out loud. It was implied. I wondered if they thought I was planning on being *in* the skit rather than just working *on* the skit. That was yet another conversation that we could only put off for so long.

As Hope headed out for her car, I felt another surge of annoyance toward her. I was the one who was supposed to be grappling with my sexuality this weekend, not her. Not that she had much grappling going on. She'd been rather blasé about the whole thing. It was possible that kissing Drea didn't come as much of a surprise to Hope. That would certainly explain the reason behind her breakup with Drew at the start of summer. A sudden interest in girls could end even the best hetero coupling.

But Hope wouldn't keep that reason secret. She blurted out the news about her kiss only hours after it had happened. Sam couldn't even bring herself to talk to me about her first time with her boyfriend, which one might consider a fairly traditional rite of passage. Definitely not something as unique as a same-sex kiss.

Or an aborted same-sex kiss.

Not that this was about me.

"You're proving to be fairly useless this morning," Blaine said, grabbing the dust cloth out of my hand. Somehow, I had managed to start cleaning that same patch of counter I'd been rubbing raw earlier without even noticing what I was doing.

"Sorry," I said. "A lot on my mind."

Mom, who was hovering, took that moment to ask if we wanted any coffee. I didn't, really. Neither did she. Mom was looking for an excuse to give Blaine and me time to talk. I requested a Vanilla Caramel Java and Mom went on her mission of lame excuse.

"If you want to go to the faire, you can," Blaine said once she was gone. "I think your mom and I can handle the store without you. That's why I gave you the whole weekend off in the first place. So you could spend the last weekend of summer with your friends. Isn't that what you've been talking about for the past two weeks?"

"It's a Renaissance Faire," I said. "How many days in a row can you go to one before you miss hearing people speak in modern slang? Or using indoor plumbing?"

"And it's got nothing to do with this Marq person?" he asked.

I stared at him blankly. I wasn't quite sure what he was suggesting. Or, more specifically, I didn't want to be right about what I thought he was suggesting.

"It's not like you to avoid people like that," he said.

Okay, *that*, I really didn't know what he was talking about. It was *totally* like me to avoid people.

"You've spent loads of time around my *über*-gay friends," he added, clueing me in.

"Oh. Hey. Whoa!" I said. "This has nothing to do with Marq's über-gayness. You know me better than that." Honestly, he knew me better than anyone in the world, including best friends and parental units. I had a sneaking suspicion that he was trying to trick me into something here. As such, I made sure to tread carefully, because our conversation was bound to be full of land mines.

"And what did you two boys really do last night?" Blaine asked. "Sneak into any clubs? Partake in some underage drinking?"

"Like you don't have friends all over town who would have already ratted me out if that happened," I said, with a telling crack in my voice. "We went to dinner. Then walked around. I was home long before the bars closed. You can ask Mom."

"Sounds . . . nice," he said.

"It was," I said.

"So, why don't you want to hang out with him today?"

"This has nothing to do with Marq," I replied. Which was partially, but not entirely, true. It had to do with a lot of things. Not the least of which being that I really was tired of the Ren Faire. It would be nice to go one day without getting locked in the stocks . . . I mean, pillory.

"Besides, I have to pick up Suze," I said.

"She's the one who's been calling and texting you all summer long, right?" He asked like he didn't know exactly who all my friends were. "She's finally coming home, huh?"

"Yes," I said.

"Wonder what she thinks she's coming home to."

"What's that supposed to mean?" I asked, though I had a fair idea what he was talking about. "She's just a friend."

Blaine nodded. "So you say. But the question is, does *she* know that she's just a friend."

Now, I was the one nodding. That was a good question, indeed.

Suze's flight was forty-five minutes late getting in. I would have known that if I'd bothered to check the flight schedule before I left the store. But I'd been so eager to get out from under Blaine's questioning gaze that I'd left a bit earlier than I had to. Which meant I got to the airport close to an hour and a half before she landed. Thankfully, I had my copy of *Fahrenheit 451* to keep me company as I waited at the luggage carousel.

After we hugged hello and got her bags, Suze regaled me with tales of her exploits in New York on the way to the nearest of the shopping/entertainment/dining complexes that were scattered about the L.A. area so we could grab some lunch. By the time we chose our restaurant and were seated, I'd learned exactly how amazing a time Suze had had interning at Hope's mom's fashion studio, Ellis Designs. Not that she hadn't told me all this during our many, many phone conversations over the summer, but her enthusiasm was more immediate in person.

I countered on the conversation, filling her in on all the happenings at the Renaissance Faire that I could think of. Really, I was looking for filler. Everything that came to my mind came out of my mouth. I had the strangest sense of foreboding that I didn't want us to run out of topics.

Suze was more excited about the faire than I thought she'd

be. Certainly more than I had been. I think she was mostly interested in taking a stroll through the House of Sandoval and comparing those dresses with the actual historical representations that she'd studied back at the New York Public Library on her last day in the city. She takes her fashion way serious. When she knew she'd be stopping by some Renaissance-themed entertainment, she got right down to business researching. But talk of the fashions of the sixteenth century could only take us so far. We finally hit a lull about the same time our dessert arrived.

"So . . . ," Suze said as she picked at the slice of chocolate cake we were sharing.

I've worked up the nerve to start conversations before in my life, so I knew all the telltale signs; the shy, furtive glances, the deep breaths, the false starts. Either she had something important she wanted to tell me or she was about to have a heart attack.

It had to be the subject I'd spent all summer hoping we could avoid. She and I had been friends for much of our lives, but we'd only gotten close after we went to the prom together. I could see in her mind how that time spent would naturally segue to the next logical step. I could also see that, unless I stopped her, I was going to have to turn her down.

I decided the best course of action was to hit her with a pre-emptive strike. "I'm so glad you're back," I said, mentally bashing myself in the head for opening that way. Then, I added, "I missed you this summer." Which only made things worse.

The look of hope I saw in her eyes just about killed me, so

I busied myself by mangling the cake with my fork. It was one of those times in life that I wished I had my own personal playwright feeding me the perfect lines. I briefly wondered how much Hope would charge to fill that role, when I noticed our stilted silence was rapidly reaching its time limit.

As Suze opened her mouth to speak, I quickly said, "You really are one of my best friends."

"Friends?" she asked.

"Just like Sam and Hope. It's like I have three sisters. Not to be confused with the play of the same name. Or the three 'weird sisters' in *Macbeth*. Or the Andrews Sisters. Although they were actual sisters, so I don't think the comparison makes any sense." At the point I was referencing girl groups from the forties, I realized I was babbling.

Luckily Suze hadn't really heard what I said. "Sisters?" she asked, before clamping her mouth shut.

"Yeah," I said, feeling redness in my cheeks. "I don't have much family." Honestly, the one "relative" I have closest to my own age is Blaine's dog. "So it's nice to think of my friends as family. And for some reason, I don't have all that many guy friends. Not anymore anyway. So it's nice to have girl friends . . . I mean, *female* friends . . ." I started blathering on about friends and family. I sounded like an ad for cellular service, but at least my babbling had taken on some sort of a structure, instead of random conversation about famous family music acts. It didn't matter. Neither one of us was listening to what I was saying at this point. I ended my spiel by shoving a forkful of cake into my mouth.

"Sisters?" she asked again.

I felt horrible, but what could I do? If she was about to ask me to be her boyfriend or something like that, I couldn't lead her on. That would be a hundred kinds of mean and just plain stupid on my part.

Then again, I could have been wrong about what she wanted to say. It was mighty presumptuous of me to *assume* that she had any feelings for me at all.

Oh, who am I kidding? I know enough about unrequited crushes to recognize what one looks like when it's aimed in my direction.

Ain't Misbehavin'

Suze and I finished our cake in silence. It had been an unprecedented weekend for me. I'd turned down two people of two different genders in two days. In less than twenty-four hours, even. And while I knew I'd made the right decision with Suze—the *only* decision, really—I was still having a nagging feeling over the whole Marq thing.

Once we'd scraped every last sliver of chocolate from the plate with our forks, I asked Suze if she wanted me to take her home. She thought about it for, like, point-five seconds and said she'd rather go straight to the faire. Personally, if my mom was as intimidating as hers, I wouldn't necessarily be in a rush to head straight home either, but she had been gone all summer. There *had* to be some homesickness. Suze then reminded me that her parents were out at some business retreat for the weekend, so the house was empty.

But, more important, I was glad that she was up for spending the afternoon with me. Don't know how I would have felt if she'd preferred to head home so she could spend the rest of the day crying over the fact that I'd shattered her dreams of ever having me for her boyfriend.

Okay, maybe a tiny, miniscule part of me would have thought it was kind of cool to have someone pining over me. I'm not proud of that itty, bitty piece of my ego, but I'd be lying if I didn't acknowledge it existed. And there was enough lying going on already. Or, if not actual lying, there was definitely some withholding of the truth taking place.

We navigated our way through the tourists back to the parking structure and Electra, turned up the volume on the iPod, and sang along with Fergie as we headed up the 405 to Sunset and then on to the coast. Odd how my two "dates" began and ended with the same soundtrack.

"Wave to the new store," I announced as we passed the shopping center.

"Li'l Beaches!" Suze said. "I *love* it."

"Totally my idea," I lied. Blaine had come up with that one. Actually, he came up with "Little Beaches." I suggested the "Li'l" part. Personally, I think it's the "Li'l" that really makes the joke sing.

Traffic was already backed up when we turned onto Malibu Canyon Road. I figured there was no way we were going to find a spot at the Country Club this late in the day, so we took the satellite parking option at Pepperdine, then shuttled it out to the Ren Faire with the masses. If I thought people dressed in Ren Faire regalia looked strange on a golf course, that was nothing compared to seeing them standing up on a bus like weekday morning commuters.

Pardon me sir, is this the bus to the bear-baiting arena?

Since we weren't with costumed people to sneak us in through the back, we had to take the main entrance. I offered to pay for Suze—you know, since I'd recently broken her heart and all—but she countered by pointing out that would totally negate her buying me lunch as her way of thanking me for the airport pickup. I didn't bother arguing, seeing as how I could spend the money I was saving on some more funnel cake. That stuff is seasonal, you know. Might as well enjoy it while I can. Especially since I hardly enjoyed the chocolate cake at the restaurant. Oh, I ate it, all right. But I didn't enjoy it.

Since I wasn't exactly in a rush to see Marq . . . or Sam . . . I toured Suze around the Renaissance Faire like I was some kind of expert on the place. As one might expect, she was particularly interested in seeing and comparing the various clothing shops. As one might not expect, whenever she saw an outfit of inferior quality, she was rather vocal about it. The third time we'd earned a hurt, yet angry, look from a woman twice our collective size, I let my eyes warn Suze off by bugging them out in her direction.

"Sorry," she giggled. "I've spent close to two months in the fashion world. Everyone there is like Marc and Amanda from *Ugly Betty*. Nobody really holds back their opinions."

A dangerous trait in Malibu, where secrets and hidden agendas are the order of the day.

"I get that," I replied. "But could you reserve your judgment for the people who can't beat us to death? I've spent too much time in the dungeon this weekend. I don't want to visit the infirmary too."

"Duly noted," she said.

It felt like everything was going to be fine with us. We'd quickly fallen back into the roles we'd been playing before any romantic tension reared its ugly head. This was good because we had finally reached the House of Sandoval and I could only handle so much self-consciousness in one afternoon.

"So, you finally showed up to help!" Sandy Sandoval said by way of greeting as she slipped a maroon cape onto my shoulders. "I'm going to have to stop giving you the freebies if you don't start earning your keep around here."

"Oh, no," I said in a deadpan. "Not that." By the time she left town, I was definitely going to have an entire Renaissance Faire outfit in my closet. I'm kind of embarrassed that it took me three days to accept that fact. Though the cape and the leather pouch were pretty cool. One glance in the nearest mirror confirmed that the cape was made for me. The jury was still out on the Elizabethan cap that was hanging back in my closet at home.

"Sandy, this is . . ." I turned to Suze only to find her gone. "Where'd she go?"

"Oh my God," Suze's voice called from inside a circular rack. "The stitching on this tunic is freakin' fierce."

Sandy's face got all excited as she disappeared into the

inerr

same rack. They didn't even bother to greet each other before they got into talking all about Renaissance fashions. I could tell that this was the most impressed Suze had been since we got to the faire. And Sandy was eating it all up. I'm sure it isn't often that she gets someone with Suze's expert eye admiring her work.

The downside was that their bonding meant that I was left alone. But not for long.

"Oh . . . hi," I said with a start when I realized that Marq was beside me. Can't imagine he ever managed to sneak up on anyone in his entire life. But there he was, standing right next to me the moment his mom disappeared.

"Oh . . . hi," he replied, mimicking my lackluster greeting. He didn't make a move to hug me for the first time since I'd met him. "Was that your *giiiirlfriiieeeend?*"

Wow. Bitter. That was surprising because we had left on good terms the night before. I couldn't imagine where the attitude was coming from.

"Um . . . that's Suze," I said, figuring he didn't need any further clarification.

"Hmmf," he said. "I expected . . . more."

Yikes.

My brain tried to come up with some bitingly sarcastic retort. My brain failed. Then my brain got all kinds of confused when Marq doubled over with laughter.

"Girl!" he squealed, mistaking my gender. "You should have seen your face. You didn't know whether to cut me down or cut me some slack. That was precious!"

"Ha. Ha."

"We cool?" he asked, holding out his hand.

I eyed his hand warily. Clearly he was planning on using it to pull me into another one of his hugs. I balled my left hand into a fist and held it up threateningly as I took his right into my own. "We're cool," I said. He got a laugh out of that, which I had sort of expected. Even on my best day, I wasn't all that much intimidating with the physical violence. I much prefer the psychological attacks.

"Sammy!" he called out. "Bry boy is here!"

Bry boy?

Sam came around the circular rack at the same moment Suze came out of it, dressed head-to-toe in Renwear. Suze's dark hair was wrapped in a green scarf that matched the dress—they called it a surcoat—tied with a hemp belt at the waist and light brown leather boots. Talk about working a look. I swear that girl was meant to live in a different time. Seeing her standing there, looking all hot in her wench's out-fit, almost made me reconsider the whole gay thing. Then I remembered it wasn't so much a choice that I had any control over, so I just admired the view without further commitment.

Her appearance stalled any showdown Sam and I were about to have as the girls exchanged their hellos and spent the next ten minutes catching up on their summer adven-tures. Not surprisingly, Sam left out the whole bit about her recent . . . connection? . . . with Eric.

Since I already knew how both girls spent their summer vacations, I busied myself by helping a customer. Not being in costume, I wasn't supposed to, but I just closed up my cape, which was effective enough at evoking the right look. I even made a sale. Technically, I made *two* sales since I rang it up wrong the first time and had to get Marq to come over to help me.

When I asked about a commission, he laughed. Which is the exact reaction that Blaine has when I ask the same question at Kaye 9.

"Hey," Sam said to me after I sent my satisfied customer on his way.

"Oh, you noticed I was here," I said. If I were a cat, my hackles would be up. As it was, I thought I heard Marq throw a hiss in my direction. Seeing how I didn't want to put Sam immediately on the defensive, I deflected my own attitude by asking where Hope was.

"Under a tree scribbling in her journal," Sam said. "You haven't figured out what she's working on yet, have you?"

"Nope," I said. "Maybe exploring her feelings for Drea."

"Yeah. How 'bout that?" Sam said.

"Yeah. How 'bout that?" I repeated. We were experiencing several levels of awkward that we didn't usually share. Understandable, since this was the first time I'd seen her since she found out I knew about her little secret. "Want to go for a walk?" I asked. The question was loaded with tension.

"It's been real busy here this afternoon," Sam said, ignoring the tent around us that had recently gotten unusually empty. "I don't think the Sandovals can spare me."

"That's okay, Sammy," Mrs. Sandoval said, popping out

from behind a rack of dresses. "Suze's going to stick around and help. She's already cataloguing the entire stock." Sandy wasn't exaggerating. Suze was elbow deep in the racks, examining every individual piece with that expert eye. "You've earned a break," Sandy continued. "Enjoy!"

"Alackaday," Sam muttered a fun word that I had no clue what it meant.

"Sorry," I said. "Missed that."

"Let's walk," Sam said with a huff as she left the tent without bothering to wait for me to follow.

The afternoon crowd had swelled considerably as the weekend wore on. It was tree to tree people as we pushed and maneuvered our way through the crowd. We got stuck behind a slow moving pirate parade for a while, which only made the walk more painfully long. I didn't have a clue where we were going, but I couldn't imagine it was going to be easy to find a place for a private conversation.

Until then, I figured we should get the preliminaries out of the way. "Missed you last night," I said, bitterly, as we dodged a family of Puritans preaching about the excesses of the faire, while they pigged out on cotton candy and mead. (The kids had the cotton candy. The parents had the mead. They weren't, like, mixing the two.) "What was it you had to do again?"

"Watch Jeremy's store for him," Sam said. "Didn't Marq tell you?"

"Um . . . no," I said. "All he told me was something suddenly came up." I was a tad annoyed I'd wasted some good energy being mad about getting blown off, if all it turned out to be was a miscommunication. Still, she could have called me. Or told Jeremy she already had plans and couldn't help him. "Why did you have to do that? And why was it so sudden? Couldn't this have come up sooner?" Okay, maybe I took some of that annoyance out on Sam anyway.

"He finally got up the nerve to ask my mom out," Sam explained. "They've been dancing around each other for the past decade. I figured the least I could do was work the register for a couple hours so they could have fun."

Damn. Here she was being all noble while I was trying to stay mad at her. Leave it to Sam to blow my whole mood by being . . . you know . . . *herself*.

I tried to work back up my proper head of steam by focusing on the idea that with Hope getting kissed, Sam getting . . . *whatever* . . . and now even Anne was getting some action, I was the only one totally alone.

Not that I didn't have options of my own, but acknowledging that would get in the way of my unrighteous indignation.

Sam was now walking kind of fast and with a purpose, forcing me to hurry as I followed. She led me to a quiet corner of the faire with a curtained doorway that led into a round open air tent-type-thing. The sign about the door read THEATRE OF THE ABSURD.

Fitting.

We were in the middle of a small outdoor amphitheater—or, I guess technically, it was an amphitheatre—with haystacks that served as seating gathered around a postage stamp of a wooden stage. Surely a firetrap. I couldn't help but grin at all the signs around the room that warned, SMOKE YE NOT.

Good advice all around.

"Why did you want to come here?" I asked.

"I knew it would be empty," she explained. "The shows here are down on Sunday afternoons so I booked it for our skit rehearsal later. It's hard for me to have a private conversation around this place without a dozen family friends listening in and spreading the word." She then folded her arms in front of her, struck an imposing pose and said, "Well?"

We were off to a *flying* start.

When I used to imagine us having this conversation, it was always with considerably less attitude on both parts. It usually took place in my kitchen with the two of us talking over huge bowls of dulce de leche ice cream, overflowing with whipped cream and hot fudge. And I was the one telling her about my first time, because naturally me being a guy, I'd totally lose it first.

Of course, that would have also meant that she was aware of my guy-on-guy leanings. But that's what made imagination fun. You got to skip to the easy parts.

In the present, Sam swung her arms out, leaned forward, and raised her eyebrows in the same way that Katherine Heigl does when the character she's playing wants the other person to start talking. *Oh, so that's how we're going to play this.*

"Were you planning on telling me that you and Eric slept together?" I asked. There wasn't any anger in my voice, but possibly a soupcon of hurt.

Okay, maybe there was some anger too.

"I never should have told you about that damn necklace," she said, sitting down on a haystack. I can't imagine that it was comfortable. Probably itchy.

"The hell?" I said. "You're going to get all indignant because you didn't keep *more* secrets from me?"

"I don't have to tell you *everything*," she said.

"But you did," I reminded her. "You told me about the necklace. You told me what it would mean when you took it off. Then you *took it off*. Then you told me nothing! Did I do something to you this summer? Is there some reason you don't want to tell me things?"

She then committed the ultimate sin by shrugging. As if that was some kind of genuine response. (Okay, maybe the "ultimate sin" was the premarital sex part. Depends on your definition of *sin*. Let's not get technical.)

Since she wasn't volunteering anything, I figured it wouldn't hurt to ask. "When did you decide to sleep with him? Did it just suddenly happen the night he came back?"

She shrugged *again*.

"Well, how long have you been thinking about doing it? All summer? Since you started going out?" How long had she been keeping those feelings from her best friend?

She tilted her head like she was considering my question. Or considering her answer. "Well, I was *thinking* about it ever since the first time I saw him take off his shirt after a soccer game."

"Okay! Ew! Ew! Don't need to hear that!"

"Ya think maybe that's why you weren't the first person I ran to tell when it happened?"

"But you could tell Hope. You could tell Hope and then tell her not to say anything to me about it?"

"She's a girl."

"Yes. And I'm a boy," I replied. "Now that we've had our gender roles assigned, what the hell does that have anything to do with anything?"

"Sometimes, it's easier," she said. "To talk. To Hope. About these kinds of things."

Wow. The wind went right out of me on that one. She has no problem talking to me about tampons and periods and other girly stuff, but with the genuinely important stuff she has a problem with me being a guy. *Nice.*

I had to sit down on that one. And yes, the haystacks were itchy.

Well, if she wanted to be all girly about it, I could be too. (Just don't tell Marq.) "So . . . is Eric *the one?*" I asked. Sam and I usually made fun of the whole concept of "the one" and people who insisted that they'd found "the one" while in high school. I mean, what are the odds that you could find the perfect person for you while you were still, technically, a child?

Seriously. I want to know.

"He's the first one," Sam said. "But don't worry. I may have gotten pregnant, but we're totally getting married."

She was joking, of course. Odd how it wasn't lightening my mood any. If we'd had this same conversation a week ago, I'd be playing right along asking to be the baby's godfather.

Then we'd slip into some really bad Marlon Brando impressions and chuckle over the whole thing.

I couldn't even manage to crack a smile. I also couldn't sit on the itchy haystack anymore. I needed to move. I got up and went to lean on a wooden post beside a SMOKE YE NOT sign. Then I crossed to the curtained exit and played with the material for a bit. I finally got annoyed with moving and settled on settling down on the edge of the stage. Seeing how it was only six inches off the ground, I had to sit with my legs straight out in front of me. Not particularly comfortable.

I cocked an eyebrow. Or, at least, I made my best attempt at cocking an eyebrow. I don't always manage to get them functioning independently of one another, and often, my look of sarcasm resembles one of extreme surprise.

"Sometimes it's just easier to talk about girl things with Hope."

"I'll remind you of that the next time I'm stuck outside a dressing room while we discuss bra sizing," I said.

"That's different and you know it," she said. "Why are you being such a hard-ass about this?"

"Because we don't keep secrets," I said.

To be clear, I truly meant this. What I was keeping from Sam wasn't a secret. It was just a facet of my personality I hadn't shared with her. It was also something I hadn't acted on. She *had* acted on her thing. Then she made the decision not to tell me about it. Totally different.

Sam performed a perfectly staged cocked eyebrow in my direction, but didn't say anything. I made a mental note to get her to teach me that sometime when there was less tension between us.

"Just so I'm clear," she said, "you don't have anything to say about me making what could have been one of the biggest decisions of my life? You're just pissed because I didn't tell you about it first?"

"Oh, I have *loads* to say about that," I replied. "Not the least of which being, why couldn't you wait until he was back home for more than one day and you knew that you even wanted to go out with him anymore? It's like you had some one night stand before he went off on vacation. But we'll deal with that later. I prefer to focus on one issue at a time. And, right now, the issue is me."

"At any point is this issue going to be me?" Sam asked.

"It would have been," I said. "It would have been all about you. It would have been about us. You could have come over. We'd talk all night. About everything." *Everything.* "But you took that from me. You stole our chance to share something real. Something more than snarking over how much we hate Holly Mayflower or what new shows we're looking forward to in the new fall season. I thought I was your best friend."

"You are," she said. "You and Hope. And Marq. And if you think just because I don't want to open up about one thing— one thing I want to keep to myself just for a bit—that it changes our friendship. Maybe you're not my best friend."

"You told *me*," I reminded her. "About the necklace. I never asked you about it. I never would have known."

"Yeah," she said. "But that was *before*. Before it happened. I didn't know back then how I was going to feel about it. All I wanted was a little time. To think about it. To figure out what I *wanted* to tell you. And you couldn't even give me that." She popped up from her haystack without another word and stormed out of the theater.

I mean, theat*re*.

An Enemy of the People

It was like that cliché about how you can be in the middle of a huge crowd and be totally alone at the same time. And, okay, the Theatre of the Absurd was empty at the moment, but I could hear the passing crowds on the other side of the wall. People laughing and shouting "Huzzah!" and all that. Yet, there I was. Alone.

Sam had Eric. She had him even when he was thousands of miles away. Hope had Drew. And then Drea. And whoever else came along next. She was outgoing in ways that I never was going to be. I was stuck behind these stupid walls I put up for myself because I was too shy or too stupid or too whatever.

Pity, party of one.

This was one of those moments that simply screamed for funnel cake. I exited the Theatre of the Absurd and went to get a snack while I turned things over in my mind. I had a lot of time for turning, since the food lines were incredibly long. Once I got my snack and moved past all the sentences in my head that began with "How *dare* she . . ." I actually managed to calm down a little. And I think the powdered sugar helped. A lot.

Now I had a decision to make. I could either let Sam get to me and go home, or move past it and go back to rehearse for the skit. If I went home, then I'd only be making things worse because I'd be bailing on my friends on top of whatever issues Sam and I were having. Which meant I'd lose the moral high ground. Besides, what was the point in going home to wallow in more self-pity? I picked myself up, brushed myself off and went back to the Theatre of the Absurd to start all over again.

Naturally, the whole gang was already there waiting for me. It wasn't even five o'clock yet.

"Where've you been?" Hope asked.

"I needed to get something from Electra," I lied.

"You've got powdered sugar on your shorts," Sam said, calling me on my lie. Neither one of us was about to apologize to the other, but we'd already moved on to the point where we could share a space without all the yelling. That was progress.

Sensing the tense vibe, Marq ran forward, clapping his hands and cheering, "Okay, kids. Here's what I had in mind for the skit."

Color me surprised that the person who doesn't go to our school was taking over from the start. And color me even less surprised that we let him.

"This Holly girl," Marq continued, "strikes me as the queenly type."

"Yeah," Sam mumbled. "Drag queen."

Marq looked at her. "Since you're in a mood, I'm going to ignore you using the term 'drag queen' as a pejorative." See, I told you he was particularly observant. Then again, he'd spent the past day with Sam, so I guess that wouldn't make it too hard to notice that there was a mood going on. "Anywho, since Holly's going to go the queen route, we need to go wench."

Sam shrugged.

Boy, those shoulders were getting a workout today.

"The girls can play serving wenches," Marq said. "You know, get down and dirty with the innuendo and suggestive staging." Headmaster Collins was going to love that. Then again, he'd already proven that he didn't get most of the jokes. "I will, of course, be mistress of the house." Marq shot a look my way. "Playing a role. Not a lifestyle. And, Bryan, you can be my master." He then let out an unconvincing twitter of embarrassed laugher and said, "I mean, master of the house. You know: comforter, philosopher, life-long—"

"I get the point," I said. "But I wasn't really planning to be in this. I was kind of thinking I could do something, you know, behind the scenes."

"I already called costumes," Suze chimed in unnecessarily.

"That's not going to work," Marq said. "We need a guy."

"But, you're a guy," I reminded him.

"No. I'm mistress of the house."

"Then, Sam can be the guy."

At least that got a reaction out of her. It was a "humph" but it was something.

"No," Marq said. "You're going to be in the skit."

"No, I'm not."

"Yes, you are."

"No," I repeated, "I'm really not."

"Yes," he insisted, "you really are."

"Look . . ." I filled him in on the horrible things that the famed producer-director-actor-writer-songwriter-choreographer Hartley Blackstone had said about my acting at the start of summer. I told him how much it crushed me. And how I hadn't really performed anything since and wasn't planning to perform anything anytime soon. It wasn't easy baring my soul like that in front of everyone, but they were all my close friends—or on the way to becoming close friends. As hard as it was, I knew they'd understand what I was saying and respect my feelings.

When I was done, Marq looked at me with sad eyes and said, "Yes, you are."

The boy is nothing if not consistent.

"You know what they say," he added. "When life gives you lemons, you've got to get right back on that horse."

I honestly didn't know what to make of him.

The argument pretty much ended there. Although, Marq did take some of my reluctance into consideration. "You don't have to wear a costume if you don't want to. We can work around it. Wear your boring normal clothes if you want." He used this as yet another opportunity to look me up and down. "Minus the hat."

"Fine," I said, removing my fedora and throwing it on the first row of haystacks. "But I am willing to wear the cape." I looked good in the cape.

"Hello-o-oh!" a ridiculously chipper voice sang as the curtain was pulled aside and Holly Mayflower entered with her entourage. It was amazing how the tone in the room, which had been growing lighter thanks to Marq, shifted right back to tension with the utterance of a single word that had more syllables than the creators of the English language had intended. Honestly, it wasn't so much the word as the person who spoke it, but it was still an impressive power.

"What are *you* doing here?" Hope and Sam both asked with matching disdain and emphasis.

Holly sauntered down the aisle, giving the haystacks a sneer. Her dual shadows, Alexis and Belinda, followed.

"We came to check out the venue," Holly said as her sneer deepened.

None of us were buying that one. Least of all, Sam. The timing was a little too perfect considering she was stopping by at the same time Sam had reserved the space for our rehearsal. "Didn't you do that on Saturday?"

"Saturday we were here to get a feel for the Renaissance Faire experience," Holly said. "Now we're here to check out the performance space."

Sam had clued us in on this the day before. Jeremy set it up so that the stage would be shipped over to school the following morning. Just the stage, back wall, and the haystack seating, I mean. It was all going to be set up on the soccer field to accommodate the larger audience. I guess the lucky ones would sit in the stands while the latecomers would get scratchy front row seats.

"Well, now you've seen the space," Sam said.

"We need to take measurements." Holly whipped out a pink tape measurer that I can only assume she'd specially purchased for this event. I can't imagine the Mayflowers had all that many tools lying about the house. "Don't let us get in the way," she added. "Rehearse your skit. It will give us a good chance to see what you all are doing. You know, so we don't do the same thing." She, Alexis, and Belinda laughed over the very thought that we could have the same ideas they did.

"Somehow, I think we'll be safe," Sam agreed.

This time, Holly shrugged. "Well, like I said, don't let us get in the way."

"You know," Marq chimed in, "this is good timing. We were *just* about to take a break."

We all went along with the lie and sat down on the stage.

Holly wasn't fazed by our work stoppage. She went about her work, directing Alexis and Belinda with the tape measurer while she recorded the dimensions of the stage, the walls, and the individual haystacks. She was measuring way more than she needed to, considering only about half the venue was coming with us. Still, the more time she spent measuring, the less time we were working on our skit. So, she was at least accomplishing something.

"We're going to have to work with this seating," Holly said. "I mean, authentic is one thing, but I have no intention of asking Daddy to sit on hay in one of his Italian suits. Not everyone's parents can live like this. Then again, I guess neither could yours. Or, well, both of yours, that is." That last part was directed right at Sam.

Personal issues aside, I never respected my friend as much as I did in that moment. Clearly, Holly had somehow figured out how Sam's dad had been related to the faire. That shouldn't have been too difficult, considering how everyone around here loved Sam so much. I'd learned firsthand how they were more than happy to talk all about watching her grow up when they thought they were speaking with one of her friends. Holly had spent much of yesterday hanging out at the House of Sandoval, so it was only natural that she would have heard something.

But Sam never let on, for a second, that Holly's ploy of bringing up her dad had been effective. Being as close to Sam as I was, I could feel it in the way her body tensed, but it was almost imperceptible to anyone else in the room, I was sure. She didn't smile to make it look like Holly wasn't getting to her. She didn't glare in a threatening way. She just sat there, as if she hadn't even heard a thing.

Disappointed that she failed to get a rise, Holly continued taking measurements before giving one last look at the stage. "Maybe we should measure that again," she said to Belinda. "Just to make sure we got everything right. I don't want to—"

"Okay," Hope said, popping up when we both saw Sam's hands clenching. She had obviously reached her limit. "You got everything you needed. You're done here."

Holly's face took on this sly smile, like we'd finally given her what she'd been waiting for. "Hope, I would have thought you, of all people, would want to make sure we worked extra hard to make sure we paid these Renaissance Faire people the proper respect by taking the time to make sure everything is perfect. You know, considering how you're all the same kind of freaks."

On that, Drea moved faster than the speed of sound. I know, because none of us made a sound until it was over. One moment, she was sitting next to Hope, and the next, Holly was laid out flat on a hay bale. I didn't even see the punch.

Golden Boy

As it turns out, none of us saw Drea punch Holly, because it didn't happen. Drea lashed out so quickly that she scared Holly into taking a step back and falling over a haystack and onto her ass. It's one of those things where your brain is like a half second behind your eyes, so by the time I processed it, the whole thing was over. Nobody had the time to react until Holly was on the ground.

Except Alexis, that is.

That girl must be the fastest draw in the west. While Belinda was tending to her fallen friend, I caught Alexis slipping her iPhone back into her pocket. I was pretty sure that, within the hour, all the Hollywood gossip blogs would have a photo of the famous Anthony Mayflower's wannabe celebutante daughter getting decked at a Renaissance Faire. Whether or not that's what happened.

Alexis didn't even bother to look ashamed when she

caught me catching her snapping the shot and the aftermath.

Holly sprang back to her feet, flanked by Belinda and Alexis. On the flip side, Drea, Hope, and Sam lined up, ready to pounce, with Suze in the background looking supportive but noncommittal. Being a guy, I wasn't sure what my role in this was supposed to be. I guess the better man would have tried to stop it before it started, but it already seemed too late. Besides, I never said I was the better man.

Just as things were about to really heat up, we experienced another mom ex machina as Anne entered the scene and saved us all from a tragic ending.

She paused in the doorway to take in the situation. "Everyone getting along in here?" Anne asked, lightly.

"That scary girl punched Holly," Belinda snitched.

Yells of protest immediately burst forth from our camp as we all tried to explain exactly what happened in overlapping conversations that could not possibly have cleared up the chain of events.

Anne did her best to smooth over the convoluted state of affairs, but things had progressed to a level they'd never reached between us and them before. We'd never resorted to fisticuffs. Or, the appearance of fisticuffs. It was particularly surprising, since Drea was new to this battle of wills. I guess some people can only be called *freak* so many times before snapping.

At least Anne didn't make us all shake hands before parting ways. She didn't even bother to find out what the fight had been about or try to discern who had been right and who had been wrong. She simply suggested that Holly and friends leave us to our rehearsal and that our energies would be better focused on working on our skits.

Taking their cue, Holly and the girls scampered off to wreak havoc somewhere else in the world. I'm sure she was more shocked by the unexpected turn of events than anyone. Not the punch part. It was only a matter of time before Holly's brand of rich-girl petulance got her decked. Those kinds of things were always happening at the trendiest night-clubs that she frequented. I was referring to how Holly lived in a world where the adults always took her side. Here she was, an apparent victim, and she was being sent on her way like she'd started it all. Which, she kind of did.

"Thanks, Mom," Sam said once the evil trio was gone. "Perfect timing as always. Holly was—"

Anne put a hand up to stop her. "I don't want to know. I just want your assurance that none of you are ever going to let things escalate to that level again. The only way to deal with the Holly Mayflowers of the world is to ignore them. They won't go away, but it's much better than letting yourself get all worked up. Drea, I especially expect that from the constable's daughter."

"Yes, ma'am," Drea said, properly chastised.

"Now," Anne said, her mood lightening, "I was actually stopping by with a happy surprise."

"What is it?" Sam asked.

"It's safe to come in now!" Anne called out toward the entryway.

The curtain parted to reveal Eric Whitman—long lost boyfriend and taker of virtue.

Sam flew down the aisle and launched herself into Eric's waiting arms. I quickly turned away, afraid of the kinds of images of the two of them together that were going to force themselves into my head. Of course, my turn took me right to Suze, who I still felt guilty over, so I continued the turn and wound up facing Marq. Nope. I made almost a full revolution by the time I focused on Drew, who had come in behind Eric.

"Hey," I said as he bypassed the kissing couple to join the rest of us.

"Nice cape," he said.

I held my hands to my hips and struck a heroic pose. "I look like Superman, don't I?"

"More like Superdork," he replied.

I fired heat beams from my eyes and disintegrated him on the spot.

If only.

Like his outfit was any better. Drew was wearing Aéropostale shorts and a Hollister T-shirt. When Eric finally released Sam I saw that he was decked out in the same labels, but in reverse: Hollister shorts and an Aéropostale T.

Talk about Superdorks. A fairly hot pair of dorks, but dorks nonetheless.

"Why was Holly covered in hay when she passed us?" Eric asked.

We all laughed while Sam filled him in on what he'd missed.

Summer had been good to Eric. After weeks on the East Coast followed by another vacation in the Caribbean, Eric was totally working the summer bronze. Doubtless, he'd managed to stick to his workout schedule even while he was gone. The way his muscles strained against the lettering in the Aéropostale logo clued me in to how aware he was of his own body. Seeing him like that, I guess I could understand why Sam had been unable to resist him physically. I just didn't understand where the emotional connection came in.

"I thought you weren't coming home till tomorrow," Sam said once the tale was told. "Why didn't you tell me?"

"Dad had a work emergency," Eric replied. "And I wanted to make it a surprise. I figured I could come by and sneak up on you in your natural habitat of the Renaissance Faire. Maybe get some insight into some of your more interesting quirks. Then I thought I'd invite you back to my place for an end of summer barbeque."

So much for my plans to hang out with Sam and Hope alone one last time before school started. Not that I thought that was going to happen before Eric had come onto the scene, considering the current atmosphere, but it was always fun to blame him for my troubles.

"And I'm glad I got here to see you in costume. You look hot," Eric said, oh-so classily, as he took in Sam's outfit. He could get away with commenting on her hotness so blatantly because Anne had slipped out during their kissing. He was right about the temperature of her outfit, though. Her breasts were more subdued than in the get-up she'd worn on Friday, but it was still rather flattering peasantwear.

I guess Sam finally realized that she wasn't dressed in her normal clothes, because she looked down at herself in shock. "You think? Really?"

Way to be secure there, Sammy.

"Cough-cough" Marq said. Just so there's no confusion, he said the words there. He didn't bother to fake the sound. That should come as no surprise, considering his general lack of subtlety. Or fakery.

"Oh, these are my friends," Sam said. She introduced Drea first, since she was closer and then added, "And this, as you may have guessed, is Marq."

"Hello, Sam's boyfriend!" Marq said as he ran from the stage with his arms wide to give Eric one of his signature hugs. I could only smile as I watched the terror on Eric's face as he realized he was about to be smothered by a guy with about half his body mass.

"Hold it," Sam said, throwing out an arm to stop Marq before he made contact. "No scaring off the boyfriend in the first three seconds." Funny how she didn't extend me the same courtesy when I'd first met Marq. But Eric *did* extend his barbecue invite to all.

"We've got to put together this skit first," Sam said. "But you can stay and watch if you want."

"Hey," I said. "Why don't you and Drew join us? We've been looking for guys to add to the cast." My intention of saying this was that we could all share a fun laugh over Eric and Drew's reactions. They weren't exactly the acting types. Seeing Eric squirm his way out of the skit was supposed to be fun. What I got was something else entirely.

"Skit?" Eric asked. "What is this skit to which yon friend refers?" Oh, he was *so* trying to impress with the Renaissance-type speak. Sam filled him in on the skit challenge with Holly, connecting it to the throw-down he'd almost walked in on. He nodded like the dutiful boyfriend while she explained where we were in the planning stage—not far—and what we were open to doing—just about anything.

For some reason, he looked to me when she was done. "What the hell? Could be fun. It's not like you have to be a real actor, right?"

"Not at all," Hope said. "That's why we asked Bryan to be in it."

For once in my life, I gave her a slap on the arm instead of the other way around. Nice to know we had progressed from the tragic circumstance of me possibly never acting again to the point where we could joke about it freely.

Yes. My own personal hell was now fair game.

"Where do we start?" Eric asked as he took the stage.

Great. Eric was already the most attractive guy in school. Nothing like sticking him on a stage to put his looks on even more of a display. What next? Shine a spotlight on him too?

"Come on, Drew," he said. "Get up here. We're going to be actors!"

I turned to my former best friend. "Does he often volunteer you for things without asking first?"

"Do you always try to make trouble where there's none?" Drew asked in response.

What could I say? The only honest response was, "Yes."

He laughed and joined his friend onstage. "So, what do we do now?" he asked.

I guess since Drew directed that question to me, it inspired everyone to look in my direction. "Who put me in charge of this thing?" I asked. "Hope's the writer." I wanted to add that Marq was the control freak that took over earlier, but I didn't want to tempt fate by putting Marq in charge. In light of our little tête-à-tête with Holly, we now needed to make extra sure that we pulled this skit off perfectly. Somehow, I didn't think that we'd have an easy time of it with Marq telling Eric what to do.

"Okay," Hope said, falling into a quick pace. "Let me think this one out." I'd never watched Hope seek inspiration on the fly before. It was kind of like watching a caged animal looking for an escape. There was a hunger in her eyes that I personally never felt about anything before. Like her life depended on her coming up with the perfect idea. It was equal parts fascinating and frightening to watch.

"Got it!" she said. "We'll do a kind of *A Connecticut Yankee in King Arthur's Court* thing. Bryan, you, Eric, and Drew will all be best friends in present day." I eyed the other guys skeptically. Talk about an acting challenge.

"Something happens . . . ," Hope continued, diving for the trunk that held our props. Nobody said anything while she dug through it, throwing things that weren't of interest to her out on the hay bales. We were all too afraid to interrupt her flow of thought and incur her wrath. Finally, she pulled out a chalice and held it up like it was the Holy Grail . . . which it could have been. Who really knew what all the props had been intended for at one time or another?

"You guys find this chalice," she said, handing it to me. "It's magic. It sends you back in time to the Renaissance where you meet me, Sam, and Suze. We're servants to the queen. And we all fall instantly in love."

"Awww," Drew and I said together in sarcastic unison.

"Shut it," Hope said. "This is where the skit turns into a farce. Since you guys don't know how things are supposed to be in Renaissance times, you do everything wrong."

"Fitting way to cover up the fact that they really don't know anything about Renaissance times," Sam noted. I wanted to thank her for stating the obvious, but I let it go.

"Right," Hope agreed. "This catches the eye of the law—"

"I'm guessing that's where I come in," Drea said, sidling up to Hope.

"The executioner," Hope introduced Drea's character with a wave of the hand. "Things look dark for our heroes, until . . ."

"Until the queen steps in to give them a royal pardon," Marq added with a curtsy.

"And . . . scene!" Hope announced.

We all burst into applause.

"Now," Sam said, "all we have to do is make it happen."

Summer and Smoke

We spent two hours working our way through Hope's plot outline and developing our basic skit. Hope made a few notes in her journal, hitting the basic plot points, but we didn't create any specific dialogue. We wanted this to be free-flowing from start to finish. A truly improvised performance on all counts.

Eric and Drew surprised me by being able to keep up with us. This shouldn't have been a shock or anything, since they were basically playing themselves, but it was always difficult getting up on a stage and trying to be convincing no matter what the role.

Trust me, I speak from experience.

Besides, they'd never done improvisation before. But they did take direction well. I guess that comes from years and years and *years* of being on sports teams. When someone tells you to do something, you do it. Me? I tend to question authority in most forms, which is why I'm so bad at organized sports.

Disorganized theater is so better suited to me, as I quickly found out.

The idea of performing in front of people again wasn't as difficult as I worried it would be. I guess because it was improv, I wasn't feeling the pressure to be all acting a role. It was also helpful that the role I was playing was pretty much me to begin with. I am glad to say that I was noticeably better at playing myself than Drew and Eric were at playing themselves.

I take my small victories where I can.

By the time we wrapped things up, we all had a good idea what we were doing and I was actually looking forward to performing the skit. And, okay, I'll admit that just having Drew and Eric on our team would give us a leg up on Holly. No one would be expecting two of the most popular guys on the soccer team to be doing an act straight out of a Renaissance Faire. And taking it seriously.

We were all feeling pretty good when we split up to pile into Eric's SUV and Electra to head back to the Whitman Mondo Malibu Dream House for dinner. We had the place to ourselves since his brother was sleeping over at a friend's and his dad was off dealing with that work emergency. I guess Mr. Whitman can afford a house on the beach because he's willing to cut his vacation short and work on the Sunday night of Labor Day weekend. I'd just hate to be the people who work for him that also have to come in and aren't as equally compensated.

"I stopped by your mom's store today," Eric said to me as he threw some hot dogs on the barbie. "Nice digs. Love the name."

"Thanks," I said. There he was, being nice again. He always made it so difficult for me to dislike him by being a good guy and all. I quickly reminded myself that Mom's new store was across the street from his house, so he didn't, like, go out of his way or anything. That made me feel better about the hostility I always tried to keep between us.

In my defense, I know it's unfair to him. It doesn't stop me from doing it, but at least I'm aware. That should be worth something, right?

"Store?" Marq asked. I filled him and Drea in on my mom's entrepreneurial endeavor, which got us talking about Marq's mom's new store in San Francisco. Which, somehow turned around to Eric asking all kinds of questions to Marq about his family and his Ren Faire life and all that.

At first, I chalked it up to Eric simply trying to make a good impression on Sam's oldest friend. Getting Marq on Eric's side would go a long way in Eric's relationship with Sam, particularly since there's always been something standing between Eric and me becoming best buds. About halfway through the conversation I turned off my skeptic-meter and finally allowed that this was just the kind of person Eric was. But I was sure I could find something else wrong with him soon enough. He'd been gone all summer, so I was a bit out of practice in exposing Eric Whitman's flaws.

Drew, Hope, and Drea (I know! Weird trio) ran across the

street to the grocery store and brought back stuff to go with the hot dogs. Drew even made sure that they didn't get anything Suze was allergic to since she has massive food issues. Then we all settled in to watch the sunset over the houses to the right of us. (*Aside:* This stretch of beach is south-facing, so the sun doesn't set over the water like on the rest of the coastline.) We even lit a campfire so that we looked just like a scene out of a beach movie . . . or an Abercrombie & Fitch catalog.

"Good hot dogs," Sam complimented her boyfriend, like it's a challenge to cook up some hot dogs. She was sitting in his lap looking all kinds of comfortable, which, I guess she was.

Sam and Eric did make a cute couple sitting there in the firelight and the fading sunlight. Not that this was the first time I'd noticed that. For all the grief I give Eric, he's not a horrible person. It's just that he always seems to be coming between me and my closest friends. First there was Drew and now Sam. Next thing you know, he'd be making a play for Marq.

I found that idea hysterical on several levels.

With Eric being away all summer, it was almost like he'd never existed. At least, I'd fallen into the trap of believing that. Sam had spent a lot of time fighting the absence by missing him and calling him and e-mailing him and doing whatever she could to keep him in her world. But the rest of the time, she had been with me. With me and with Drew.

All in all, it had been a pretty good summer. Mom's new store opened huge. I was back to being friends with Drew again. Sam and I had been hanging out more than ever. Okay, being told I sucked as an actor was a harsh way to start the summer, but that was so many weeks ago that it hardly counted. And if my recent performance rehearsing our skit was any indication, maybe the acting thing wasn't entirely dead to me.

And here we were on what was effectively the last night of summer vacation—any Labor Day you have to spend at school doesn't count as vacation—and I was spending it with my closest friends. Though things were kind of strained between me and Sam, even watching her hanging all over Eric couldn't ruin my mood.

No. But I could. Serves me right for being so damned observant.

Wait for it. It will come to you soon enough.

I wasn't the only one who'd fallen into an introspective silence. Maybe the fire was hypnotic, because most of us were silently staring into the flames. For some, it had been a long day, so that was understandable. Suze had started her day on an entirely different coast and had experienced both a sunrise and a sunset on both sides of the country, a realization that she shared with us as the sun finally sunk behind the houses. She and Drew had their heads together in hushed conversation afterward. I couldn't tell what they were talking about—because of the hushed part—but it seemed comfortably relaxed from my perspective on the other side of the flames.

Sam was still in Eric's lap. I think they were whispering sweet nothings-I'd-want-to-hear. I'd already spent enough time silently observing them, so I moved on to the next part of our circle where Hope and Drea sat without speaking at all. They were both lost in the fire. To the outside observer, it seemed innocent enough, but I could see that their hands were slowly sliding toward each other in the sand. Whatever it was that resulted in their kiss the night before wasn't looking to be a one night thing.

Which brought me to Marq.

I hadn't intentionally planned to sit beside him, but there we were. Paired off like everyone else in the circle. Funny how that happens.

I turned to Marq in the fading sunlight and said, "Take a walk with me."

He got this cute confused look on his face, but didn't say anything. He just sprang up to his feet. "We'll be back," I announced to no one in particular as we started our way down the sand.

We walked along the water's edge in silence for a bit. I suspect it was more that I was walking in silence. He was just walking in anticipation, waiting for me to say something. Of course, Marq Sandoval can't go without speaking for too long. Once it was clear I wasn't about to get around to the reason for our unplanned sojourn, his mouth went into overtime.

"O-M-G!" he started with my favorite spelling word. "Is that?"

"Is what?" I asked, looking in the direction he was pointing. And when I say "pointing" I mean his entire arm shot out and his body was leaning in the direction of one of the sweetest houses on the beach.

"In the hot tub?" he asked. "Is that? It can't be."

But it was. One of Hollywood's biggest starlets sharing a dip with not one, but *two* hunky, unknown—and apparently *undressed*—guys. If only Alexis were here with her camera phone. "Yep," I said, "that's her. America's Sweetheart."

"Aka Sam's boyfriend's neighbor," Marq said.

"'America's Sweetheart' is easier to say."

"When Sam said she was friends with the rich and famous—"

"We're not all rich," I quickly corrected. Okay, true . . . we didn't live in mobile homes and make our own clothing, but we also didn't all have houses on the sand. My house was way up in the hills with only a glimpse of the Pacific through the trees. "Or famous."

"No need to get all defensive," Marq said. "I'm just saying . . ."

I wasn't being defensive. Just nervous. We'd gotten to the small cove that I wanted to take him to. It always reminded me of that part of the beach where Sandy and Danny frolicked in at the opening of *Grease*. It may have been, for all I know. Malibu is used for a lot of location filming.

That's about the point that I was struck by an odd thought.

"What?" Marq asked. I guess he saw it on my face.

"It's just . . . ," I said. "Your parents. They're Sandy and Daniel. Sandy and Danny?"

"Yeah," Marq said. "That's why Mom likes the Sandy nickname. And it's why Dad prefers to go by Daniel. They're weird, but I love them,"

I knew what he meant. So many people I knew were weird—or, let's say *unique*—but I loved them all in my own way. Who's to say that love has to be logical? We may not choose who we love, but we could choose how we love. Just because someone might not be our first choice, doesn't mean he can't be *a* choice. Especially if he's going to be leaving town in a couple days to move to San Francisco.

You see where I'm going with this, right?

"You didn't bring me on this twilight walk to talk about my parents, did you?" he asked.

"No," I said, checking to make sure that we had this corner of the beach to ourselves. It was the perfect time. The perfect setting. "I kind of wanted to do this." I slowly leaned forward, closing my eyes and the distance between our lips. All the nerves in my body were tingling like they do in some trashy romance novel. Probably because of the chill to the night air off the water. Either way, I let it work for me.

I felt his hand on my chest. Pressing against me.

Pushing me away?

My eyes blinked open and flitted down to that offending hand. "I thought you wanted—"

"I did," he replied, with a sad nod. "Still do. But you don't."

"But I—"

"Looked both ways before you proceeded to kiss," he said. "Checked to make sure no one was watching. No one would know about it."

"That's not why—"

"Maybe it is," he said. "Maybe it isn't. Either way, I'm feeling like there's more to this kiss than just, you know, a kiss."

"Such as?"

"Think you were the only one who noticed everyone paired off back there? If a boy's going to kiss me, I prefer it to be me he's kissing, not just the first guy that comes along so he won't be alone."

"That's not . . ."

But it was. Kind of. I mean, all my friends seemed to be making these major moves in their lives. And I couldn't even find a way to come out of the closet because I was more worried about the big production of *coming* out than, say, the reality of life *being* out. It was getting to be kind of like those bridezillas. You know, the ones who make it all about their wedding day, without even thinking of the marriage that comes afterward. It was like that with me, but in reverse. I was so freaked about being, like, the Anti-Gayzilla that I was overcompensating for *not* coming out.

Coming back to the fire with a boyfriend would have been the easy way. It just wouldn't be fair to the boyfriend who I was using solely as a prop. It wouldn't really be fair to me, either.

"Sorry," I said, both to Marq and myself.

"No prob," he replied much more brightly than I would have if I'd been in his sandals. "Care to talk about what's bugging you? I'm getting the impression that I'm not meeting you on your best weekend ever."

"That obvious, huh?" I asked, pulling up some sand beside him.

"Sam's always writing me about her *amazing* friend Bryan and how *amazing* he is," Marq said.

"I'm not living up to expectations?"

"Oh, I think you're pretty amazing," he said. "I don't get the feeling that Sam thinks that right now."

I dug my Chucks into the sand. I was going to be shaking them out for weeks to come, that wasn't the part bothering me. I was about to cross a line. Marq had known Sam way longer than I did. He was probably the one person in the entire world who could help me get a handle on why she was being so weird with me since she'd slept with Eric. The thing was, it wasn't like my place to out her on that, either. I had to enter into this conversation carefully or I could make an awkward situation between me and Sam deadly for us.

"You know about Sam's necklace, right?" I asked, testing the waters to see how much I had to reveal and how much Marq could figure out on his own . . . with maybe a gentle push in the right direction. "The unicorn one she always used to where?"

"The one her dad gave her?" Marq asked.

"What?"

"The silver one," Marq said. "Florella, this crazy gypsy woman who was already ancient when we were littlies designed it for Sam when she was born."

"I met her," I said, still reeling from the revelation. It made total sense. One of Sam's parents most likely had gotten it for her, considering how she'd had it since before she was getting an allowance.

Marq nodded. "It was this special design. Exactly matched the unicorn in her dad's family crest. He gave her that way back when we were itty, bitty things. It's, like, the only thing of his that she still has."

Clearly, he didn't know about the purity pledge linked to the necklace. And clearly, *I* didn't know just how messed up Sam was about her dad leaving. I mean, she takes off the one thing her father gave her after she loses her virginity? That's all kinds of complex. Like Oedipus . . . or Electra actually. (*Aside:* Not the car, the character from Greek mythology. Has her own play and everything.)

Marq was entirely unaware of the major revelation I was making there in the sand beside him. He continued, "I figured she took off the thing because she was finally ready to let her dad go. You know, accept that he was never coming back."

Or that she was at a stage in her life where she didn't need him to come back. I'm no psychologist, but maybe Sam was putting a wee bit of unnecessary pressure on her relationship with Eric. And maybe her best friend was making things a whole lot worse with his jokes and comments at her boy-friend's expense.

Whoops.

"You know how she is with her fantasy stuff and symbolism and all that," Marq added, unknowingly twisting the knife in my gut a bit further. "You okay?"

I thought about his question. It shouldn't have been that difficult to answer, but it was. I sighed. "I think so. But, can you do me a favor tomorrow? It will make my life a lot better."

Picnic

Labor Day.

This break from school did not quite end—or begin, really—in the way I'd imagined it would. Sure, the middle was fine. Not quite interesting enough to write about, but I'd had some fun. This was supposed to be my last big summer adventure. Next year it would be all about getting ready for college. Starting my second act. I'd been planning to have one last hurrah.

Instead, I got a lame huzzah.

And here I was about to step onstage in front of an audience for the first time since a famous Broadway director-producer-etc. tore me to shreds.

Is it any wonder I couldn't manage to get out of bed?

Is it any wonder Mom didn't even try to wake me herself?

She sent Blaine instead.

"Man, your dad is pissed," he said by way of greeting. He

dropped down onto the bed beside me, jostling me fully awake. This was his version of an alarm, I guess.

"What did you do to him?" I asked, playing along.

"Not me, buddy boy," he said. "You. How do you expect him to come home to see you in a show if we don't learn about the show until the night before said show."

"Show?" I asked, not entirely sure what he was talking about. I couldn't have been *that* asleep. I'd been lying in bed staring at the ceiling for a good fifteen minutes before he came in. "I don't have a clue what you're talking about."

"This Renaissance Faire show you're in today at the picnic."

"It's just a stupid skit," I moaned, turning my back to Blaine.

You'd think by now that I would have learned this to be a bad move.

A moment later I felt the sheets being pulled off me.

"And how would you feel if I'd been sleeping naked?" I asked. Like that was ever going to happen. I was in my usual sweatshorts and T-shirt bedtime ensemble.

"Like I didn't used to bathe you and wipe your butt when you were a baby," he said.

"I'm up!" I said, though my body stayed down.

"The next thing coming off the bed is the fitted sheet with you on it," Blaine warned.

"Okay. I'm really up," I said, sitting up.

"Good," he said. "But next time, let your dad know. Him being so far away just makes it worse when he hears about things like this."

"Sorry," I said, making a mental note to call Dad later and

apologize. It's not his fault his job smuggling contraband (or whatever it is he does) takes him to third world countries. He usually makes a big deal about coming home to see me perform. But really, this was just a stupid skit. Nothing to even e-mail him about, much less call him and ask him to fly home for. Guess we all have our daddy issues. Even daddies.

That got me thinking of Sam again. I worried that Marq would forget to run that errand I'd asked him about the night before. Not that he was all that flaky about important stuff, but I liked to worry about things. It kept my mind off obsessing about the skit. And getting up in front of hundreds of people to perform again.

Yikes.

I pulled the sheet up over my head.

Blaine pulled it right back off me. "Anything you want to talk about now? You know, there *was* a time when you used to confide in me."

I thought about that. The reality was that I already knew what he would say about most of my dilemmas. And, to be honest, the biggest one was going to be handled once I got to school. If I didn't chicken out first.

"Nah," I said. "My other gay friend helped me work through most of it."

He gave me a sideways glance but didn't say anything. Unlike Marq, Blaine didn't like being marginalized as the "gay friend," but he was in touch with me enough to know what I was saying.

He's perceptive like that.

I hope to be too, someday.

"We're rolling out in twenty minutes," Blaine said. "With or without you."

Like I couldn't take Electra. Then I remembered how packed the parking lot at Orion got on the day of the Back-to-School Picnic and checked the clock. Unless I wanted to hike a mile, uphill, to get there I had to get my butt in gear.

I think I surprised us all by being ready in fifteen minutes. The process was helped by my already having my back-to-school outfit picked weeks ago. I'd bought it while on vacation in Vancouver. The added bonus is that I'd get to debut it onstage. Thankfully, it went well with my cape.

Blaine pulled into a spot at the back of the parking lot, preferring to give the catering trucks by the entrance a wide berth. We made our way through the trees along the path that led to the soccer field, where the picnic was getting into full swing. The tone was set early as we entered the field of play where Jeremy—in full Ren Faire regalia—welcomed parents and students to the grounds, handing out paper crowns for the guys and tiaras for the women.

"How now, young Master Stark?" Jeremy said when we reached him.

"You've got to be kidding me," I said when he shoved a paper crown in my hand.

"The headmaster paid us extra to throw in this stuff," Jeremy explained. "Wear it. It goes with your cape." Just to be clear, I wasn't wearing the cape yet, but I did have it draped over my shoulder.

I introduced Mom and Blaine to Jeremy, then gave them the scoop on his burgeoning relationship with Anne after we were a short distance away. They both gave me grief about gossiping, but were glad to hear that Anne had found someone all the same. Not that the relationship had much potential since Jeremy was going to be off to the next faire stop in a couple weeks, but it was something.

"Well, go off and have fun," Blaine said from under his paper crown. He was one of the few adults wearing one. "We'll mingle with the old fogies."

A scan of the picnic area/soccer field revealed that I was the first of my closest friends to arrive. I would have thought Sam and Anne would be there with Jeremy, but maybe they were coordinating things back at the faire. Several jugglers I recognized were standing by the stands performing for the growing crowd of parents and students. Swashbuckling swordsmen, step dancers, and bagpipers were all on the bill for the day too. Since Labor Day was supposed to be very busy at the Renaissance Faire, Jeremy had worked up a rotating schedule to keep the picnic stocked with fresh performers while not emptying out the fairgrounds at the same time. I figured that Headmaster Collins had offered a pretty farthing to get the faire to spare people.

"Where's Sam?" Holly asked in place of a polite hello. She'd come up behind me, so I hadn't had the proper time to hide. When I turned, I was surprised to find her with a larger than usual entourage. Sure, Alexis and Belinda were right on her

Prada heels, but they were also accompanied by Gary McNulty and Jason MacMillan.

All of them were dressed in period costumes that I'm guessing Sandy had relented to outfit them in. We'd been right in assuming Holly was going the queenly route for her skit. She was adorned in what had to be the contents of her mom's entire jewelry box. I was kind of surprised she didn't have a security guard trailing a few steps behind her.

"Monkey Boy!" I said, ignoring Holly completely. "Jason! How are you guys?" I hadn't seen either of them since the Summer Theatrical Program ended. Jason had won the guy's part and went along with Holly to New York to study under Hartley Blackstone. Gary . . . well, I didn't know where he'd been all summer. Considering he had enough energy that the name Monkey Boy suited him, I figured whatever he did, he had fun doing it.

I didn't have a chance to find out what that was, because Holly cut the guys off before they could get a word out. "Sam?" she asked again. "She is coming, right?"

"She wouldn't miss it for the world," Hope said. I swear I need eyes in the back of my head. People do have a tendency to sneak up on me. I need to be more alert. When I turned, I was surprised to see her in normal clothes. Well, normal for Hope, I mean. She was in black jeans, black t-shirt, and black sneakers with pink laces that matched her pink contacts. What I mean is that she wasn't dressed as a Ren Faire character like Holly's team.

"Sam's putting some finishing touches on the sketch along

with her Renaissance Faire friends," Hope said. "I mean *freaks*. Isn't that what you called them before you wound up with your ass in the grass?"

"Thanks for reminding me," Holly said ominously as she turned and stalked off with Alexis and Belinda. It bothered me that she didn't stick around to sling insults awhile longer.

Gary and Jason stayed behind a second to shrug and shake their heads in resignation before exiting, stage left. At least they knew they were teaming with the devil on this skit and didn't take it too seriously.

"Where've you been?" Hope asked as she started walking back toward school.

"I've been here," I said. "Where you found me."

"Didn't you get my message?" she asked. "We're all meeting in the dressing room."

"You know my cell phone doesn't get reception here," I reminded her.

Hope rolled her eyes. "We have got to get you on my plan. But it's good because I wanted to talk to you privately anyway."

Of course that would be the cue for Drew and Eric to come up from the parking lot and join us.

"Tell me again why I agreed to do this?" Drew asked me as he came up beside me.

"Because your leader told you to?" I suggested.

That comment went over like a lead hot-air balloon.

"Correct me if I'm wrong," Eric said. "But, wasn't this all *your* idea?"

Yeah, but I'd been making a joke. I didn't say that out loud, but I was pretty sure that Drew had figured it out. He was squinting his eyes in my direction as if trying to let me know that he was on to me. And that he would get back at me on some future occasion.

"I was hoping we could go over this one more time before we have to go onstage," Drew said.

"We will," I assured him. "Sam will probably make us go over it a dozen times. Don't know if you've ever noticed, but she can be kind of obsessive about this acting stuff."

"You don't say," Eric said, in an attempt at joking cama-raderie. Don't know why, but I flashed him a smile as if we were friends and on the same page.

We went in at the main entrance by the Saundra Hall Auditorium (aka Hall Hall). The hallway was empty since all the action was happening over at the soccer field. When we reached the dressing room, Hope sent Drew and Eric on inside, but she held me out in the hall for that mysterious talk she wanted to have.

"I need your help," she said. "I've been working on a play. A one act. My first one act. I had the idea back in New York. I wanted to finish it before school started and . . . well . . . I did."

"A play?" I asked, a few seconds behind. For as long as I'd known her, Hope was always writing poetry. This was the first time she'd branched out into a new genre. Okay, she had writ-ten a few monologues here and there, but a one act had some substance. Not as much as a full play, but you've got to work up to these things.

"I stayed up all night polishing the final draft," she told me.

"That's great," I said, though I was wondering when she'd last slept.

She checked around to make sure we were alone. "I gave a copy to Mr. Randall this morning. I told him that if he liked it, I wanted it to be in the Fall One-Act Festival."

"You *told* him? You didn't . . . *ask* him?" Sure, other students in the school liked to tell teachers what they could and could not do. Our drama teacher certainly gets an earful around the school show each year. But me and my friends have never exercised that particular ability. Mainly because Sam's mom and my parents don't wield the kind of financial power to back it up. Hope didn't do it mainly because her stepsisters often *did*. That was usually reason enough not to do something.

"I'm sick of the Mayflowers running this school," Hope said. "My father can totally beat up her father, legally speaking. The way to succeed at Orion is to throw around your weight." She grabbed her breasts for emphasis. "And I've got a lot of weight to throw around."

I couldn't help it. I laughed. It was funny.

"You want to know what else I told Mr. Randall?" she said.

I braced myself. "Not particularly."

"That I want you to direct."

I Am a Camera

There was quite the silence that followed. A long, protracted silence while I tried to figure out what Hope was thinking by suggesting that I could direct her play if it was included in the Fall One-Act Festival. No student had ever directed anything more than scenes for class at Orion. It just wasn't done. To have a student director was the kind of power play that would shake up the Drama Geeks to the core.

Which, granted, would be a good enough reason for some to accept the challenge.

"That is," she said, "if you *want* to direct it. I have a copy of the play for you in my locker. Obviously, you should read it before you decide."

Hope was looking at me with such . . . well . . . *hope.*

She was the second person this summer who had suggested I try my hand at directing. Maybe there was something to this idea.

"Read it?" I asked. "Hope, I've read everything you've ever written. Well, everything you've *allowed* me to read. And I've loved every single piece. How could I not love your first play? Of course I'll direct it."

And then Hope did something entirely out of character. She bounced up and hugged me.

Which is how Sam found us when she came out of the dressing room. "Okay, *this* I cannot handle," Sam said.

"Bryan's going to direct my play," Hope explained as she released me.

"What play?" Sam asked.

"The one I wrote," Hope said in a "duh" tone.

Sam looked at me for clarification and I just shrugged.

I shrugged at *her* for a change.

Sweet victory!

"Well . . . congratulations," Sam said. "Hope, you need to get into costume. We're going on soon."

Hope did something else out of character, grabbing my hands and giving them a squeeze while she squealed, "See you soon!" And then she skipped—SKIPPED!—to the dressing room. We stood in stunned silence as the door slammed shut behind her.

"You'll have to fill me in on that later," Sam finally said.

"Oh," I replied nonchalantly, "you're speaking to me now?" Yeah. That wasn't the way I had intended to start this conversation. I was hoping to have run into Marq by now. That would have made things much easier.

"I was never *not* speaking to you," she said. While we both went over that double negative in our heads to make sure it meant what she thought it meant, she made it even more convoluted by adding, "I was just not telling you something."

"I get that," I said. My eyes were naturally drawn to that bare spot on her neck. "And I get why you maybe wanted to keep it more to yourself." I considered telling her that I understood the whole convoluted part about that necklace coming from her father. But, honestly, she might not have made the connection herself. To her, the unicorn might simply have been a symbol of purity without any deeper meaning. Either way, standing in the hallway outside the dressing room was not the place for that kind of conversation. It would have been a perfectly fine place for me to do what I'd intended, if only I'd met up with Marq.

I considered asking her to wait while I ran into the dressing room, but there was something else we needed to cover first. There were still some hurt feelings. Mainly mine. "It *was* a pretty big something, though."

"And you've never kept any pretty big somethings from me?"

"Never," I said in my best imitation of that famed liar, Pinocchio. Just because I was thinking that the conversation might wind its way around to me, didn't mean that I was prepared for it when it did.

Naturally, Sam was playing the part of Jiminy Cricket so, you know, it *did*. "Then you're either lying to me or you're lying to yourself."

Why was there never a whale around to swallow you when you wanted one?

You see, we were finally talking about it. In our own little way, yes. But we were dealing with the one thing that I never felt the need to say before. The thing I still wasn't sure that I needed to actually tell. "If you honestly thought I was lying to myself," I said, "somehow I doubt you'd call me on it like that."

"True," Sam replied.

"So, you know?" I asked.

"I've thought it."

"Me too."

"But you never said anything," Sam said.

"Never seemed to be a reason."

"Why won't you let me use that excuse with what I did with Eric?"

"Because," I said, "that's a big moment. Something you *did*. Something you kept from me. I haven't had a big moment. I'm just me. So, there's nothing to tell."

"Some people would say otherwise."

"I'm not some people," I reminded her.

"True."

Then there was a long pause. I worried that it was possible that we were talking about two different things. That I was coming out to her, but she was all thinking that I was saying that I had a secret passion for Renaissance Faires that I was too afraid to tell her about before. There was an easy way to clear it all up, but I didn't see much point in it.

"So . . . ," Sam said.

"So what?" I replied.

"Aren't you going to say it?"

"Say what?"

"The one phrase that seems to be missing from this conversation. Two words. Starts with *'I'm.'*"

I paused to consider that phrase. If *she* knew and *I* certainly knew, then why was a proclamation necessary? "Wasn't planning it."

She nodded in understanding, even though she didn't.

I quickly headed off *that* conversation. "No, I don't have issues. I just don't plan to make it an announcement. It is what it is."

Sam surprised me by reaching out and pulling me into a hug. One of those nice, friendly hugs that reminds you no matter how many misunderstandings you have, or even full-blown fights, you've always got a pair of arms where you can find solace. Although with Sam in her Renaissance Faire dress, up all that close to me . . . the breasts were a wee bit . . . *aaagghhh*.

It would have been a nice moment to end on. (Minus the *aaagghhh*, that is.) Fade to black on the hug and all. Very Hollywood musical.

Naturally, Holly Mayflower had to come up and ruin it. Along with her entourage—the entourage that had increased by one.

"Headmaster Collins!" Sam said, pushing me away like he had caught us in the middle of something that she and Eric would have been doing.

"Samantha," he said and I watched Sam shudder. "Can I see your entire group out here?"

Sam looked to me worriedly, then back to the headmaster.

"Sure," she said. When she opened the door, we all heard laughter and fun conversations going on inside. Sam quickly put a stop to it by calling in and telling everyone to come out.

One by one, our group filed out into the hall. Suze and Hope were in their wench outfits. Drea had on her executioner's robes, complete with hood. Drew and Eric had changed into T-shirts with the largest Abercrombie & Fitch logos on them I'd ever seen. I briefly wondered if they were making fun of themselves, or if it was something Hope had put them in.

Naturally, Marq was saved for last. The faces on the headmaster and everyone in Holly's group were just adorable when they realized that the girl in the huge gold dress and powdered wig that stretched three feet into the air was, in fact, a boy.

"Is that all?" the headmaster asked.

"Isn't that enough?" Holly mumbled.

The headmaster ignored her, focusing on Drea. She struck quite the imposing figure, dressed for death. "Please remove your hood," he instructed.

Drea did as she was told.

The headmaster looked us all over, before motioning to Marq and Drea. "You two do not attend Orion Academy, correct?" Considering it was part of the headmaster's job to know every spoiled student at Orion by sight, I don't know why he was even bothering to pose it as a question.

It soon became even more pointless when Anne came running up with Jeremy on her heels. "They're kids from the

Renaissance Faire," she quickly explained, clueing in to the situation. "Is something wrong?"

"I'm afraid they cannot perform in the skit," Headmaster Collins said to Anne, ignoring our group. "In fact, I am going to have to ask them—sorry that I am to do it—to leave."

Once we negotiated our way through his odd sentence construction and figured out what he was saying, we all exploded in protest. Even Gary and Jason joined in, despite their not knowing Marq and Drea . . . and that they were supposed to be on Holly's side. Holly didn't like that one much, and she made sure they knew it with her devil eyes.

Anne put up a hand to quiet us all. "Headmaster Collins, when you spoke to me about this the other day, you never said anything about these skits performed solely by our students. I thought the whole point was to give everyone a better understanding of Renaissance times. You couldn't ask for better performers than Marq and Drea, here."

"That was the intention, yes," the headmaster said. "And what you say may certainly be true. But I have a responsibility to the students and their safety. I cannot allow someone on this campus who has attacked one of our students."

Shocked faces all around. Not mine, mind you. I saw where this was going even before the iPhone made its appearance.

"Show them, Alexis," Holly said.

So I'd been wrong. Alexis hadn't snapped the shots for some gossip site. Or maybe she had, but then Holly found out and came up with a way to put the pictures to better use. The iPhone in question came out of Alexis's purse. She scrolled through the commands and held the screen out for everyone to see. It showed a shot of Drea coming at them. A quick click revealed Drea nearly on top of Holly. A second click and we had an awesome image of Holly flat on the ground. But even though the image was awesome, the inference made from it was not.

"Clearly you can see for yourselves that she attacked me," Holly said.

"Except for the part where the attack happened," Hope pointed out, pointlessly. "Funny how that particular picture is missing from your slideshow."

"My pictures speak for themselves," Alexis insisted.

It was only the headmaster's presence that was keeping a full-on battle royale from raging in the hall. Sure, Alexis's pictures could tell a story, but the thousand words they were using were the wrong ones.

Seeing as how I could speak for myself better than any photo, I did. Since I'm usually the least confrontational in the bunch, this surprised everyone almost as much as it surprised me. "Headmaster Collins," I said. "Sir. I was there. Holly fell over one of the hay bales. Drea didn't touch her. I swear, that's the truth."

Hope, Sam, Suze, and Marq all nodded their heads in agreement. Even Eric and Drew were nodding along, though they weren't even there. They'd been outside the aptly named Theatre of the Absurd at the time. Funny how Anne didn't bother to point that out.

"That may be," Headmaster Collins said, "but I have a

report that a student under my charge was attacked. It would be improper for me to allow the alleged attacker to remain on campus. At the very least I could not allow her to participate in the performance. That would not send a good message to the student body."

Or their parents, I added in my mind.

"I don't think *any* outsiders should be allowed to take part in the skits," Holly added, oh-so helpfully, with a glare in Marq's direction. "I know that would make me feel much better about this whole thing."

I could hear the gears grinding in the headmaster's head. I was pretty sure that he was adding something onto the end of her sentence like, "So I don't have to go running to Daddy." I nonchalantly stepped to my right and started unlacing the back of Marq's dress. It was going to take some time to get him out of the getup. Might as well start now.

"That's very generous of you, Ms. Mayflower," Headmaster Collins said. Drea's and Marq's jaws dropped upon hearing that, but the rest of us had expected it. Sam even came over to help me work out a nasty knot in the laces. "I think if Ms. Lawson agrees, we can put an end to this whole sordid event."

"Sure," Sam said as we undid the knot.

"Sammy!" Marq protested.

"Thank you, headmaster," Anne said, quickly, to cut off whatever Marq was about to do. The headmaster nodded like he had done something all noble and left the hall with a smile, secure in the knowledge that his position was safe for another day. Or another hour at least. There were plenty of other

Holly Mayflower types at our school who could raise just as much a stink as the original. I couldn't imagine how hard it was for the headmaster to navigate his way through the potential minefield that filled every day in his job. Then again, judging by the suit he was wearing and the car he drove, he was more than adequately compensated for it all.

"Now I really can't wait to see your skit," Holly said as she turned and stalked off with her entourage. Gary and Jason were kind enough to give us apologetic smiles before they left. Heck, even Belinda threw in a shrug that said, "What can you do?"

Once they were gone, Marq finally burst. "Sammy, how can you let her get away with that? She's ruined our skit."

"Marq, you've been at Orion for less than an hour," Sam explained. "The only way to beat a Mayflower around here is by showing her up onstage. Let her think she's ruined our skit. It'll just makes things better when we perform circles around hers. All it's going to take is a couple modifications. Hope, you'll need to play the executioner."

"On it," Hope said, grabbing a confused Drea by the hand and pulling her into the dressing room to change clothes.

At that point, Sam looked to me. "Now, Bryan, I know you don't get the whole Ren Faire deal. But being in costume onstage is a whole different thing."

Don't think I didn't see where this was going. "No!" I said. "No. No. No way. No how."

"But we need the ending to stay the same," Sam said. "It puts a cap on the whole performance. The crowd will love it."

Though some of the others were a bit slow on the uptake, Marq was right there with Sam, trying to slip off his queenly robes right there in the middle of the hallway. "She's right, Bry, you would be perfect. Remember, it's just a costume, not a lifestyle."

But it was a lifestyle. A lifestyle of stereotypes that even my friends couldn't avoid. You'll notice that, of the three guys in the hall, I was the one they turned to. And that's when I realized, that was the best excuse of all for me not to do it.

"Yeah, me in a dress would get a laugh," I acknowledged. "But come on! I'm a Drama Geek. How shocked do you think the audience will be? Now, if you want to go for the big laugh . . . if you *really* want to shock people . . . we need to give them something unexpected . . ."

My face broke into a scheming grin as I slowly turned my head . . . toward soccer-stud/class-president/blond-god/taker-of-a-young-maiden's-virtue, Eric Whitman.

All's Well That Ends Well

"Forsooth," Holly's voice echoed out over the stands. "Methinks thou doth protest too much, thy fair lady. Fie! Fie! By the beauty of Venus! Now, by my faith!"

Sam rolled her eyes my way from our spot behind the stands. "It's like she swallowed a Renaissance dictionary but doesn't know how to use it. She's not making any sense."

"Yeah," I said, "but the audience is eating it up."

Laughter burst from the stands. I wasn't sure what had just happened onstage since I couldn't see it from where we were standing, but I was pretty sure they were laughing with her and not *at* her.

"She's going to be even more impossible to deal with now,'" Sam said.

I nodded my head solemnly. It was almost too impossible to imagine.

But that's when *it* happened.

"Marry, good sir. Wilt thou mar—"

Silence.

Blessed silence.

Sam and I looked at each other. Then we looked at all our friends around us.

"You think she forgot her line?" Hope whispered.

It seemed unlikely. Even if Holly had forgotten her line, she would have covered for herself. She's the last person I'd ever expect to freeze onstage. Or, at the very least, Jason or Gary would have jumped in to save her. But the silence was stretching on for a remarkably long time.

"Bryan, go see what's up," Sam said.

"Why me?" I asked.

She rolled her eyes. "Because you're not in costume."

I looked down at the Abercrombie & Fitch shirt I was wearing and had to disagree. But I went anyway. Making my way around the stands, I heard some mumbling from the audience. I worried that something serious had happened and quickened my pace. As I got to the front, I finally heard Holly's voice again. Only it was much, much softer.

It seems that karma had finally come up and bit Holly in the butt. The sound system had cut out and she was doing everything in her power to ensure that the show went on by screaming her lines at the top of her lungs. Unfortunately, the breeze was carrying her shrill voice out through the trees and over the ocean instead of toward the stands where everyone could hear her.

Every once in a while I believe in a higher being. This was

one of those times. Granted, my higher being was of the vindictive variety, but this should come as no surprise.

Holly tried to overcompensate by screeching even louder and practically blew out her vocal cords. Jason's quick thinking took over and he started wrapping up the skit in pantomime, but the damage was already done. The polite applause that came at the end was more for their perseverance than their performance. I quickly ran back behind the stands to make my report, but someone had beaten me to it. Jimmy Wilkey, Orion's intrepid stage manager-technical guru had already run back there to fiddle with the sound system, since he was getting nothing from the sound booth in the stands above.

To say that our cheers drowned out the audience would be a *slight* exaggeration, but you could tell we weren't all that upset. Especially when the headmaster suggested a brief pause in the performances to fix the system.

Oh, he offered Holly that chance to redo her skit as well, but she refused. Seeing how her throat was all scratchy, she had a much better time playing the martyr than replaying the scene.

In the meantime, we set up our scene, careful to make sure that Eric remained hidden. We got into our opening positions and waited for the green light. The best part was that it only took a couple minutes to fix things.

"I got it working, Bryan," Jimmy said as his voice projected out over the soccer stands.

"Yes, I see that," I replied. "Hear it too."

"Whoops," he said, still projecting. "Just one quick—" The sharp squeal of feedback—a sound somewhat reminiscent of Marq's voice when he's at his most excited—blasted from the speakers out over the unsuspecting audience. "Got it!" Jimmy exclaimed.

"Thanks," I said as Drew and I prepared to take the stage with full confidence that it was going to take a lot of work for our performance to be any worse than Holly's.

"You ready?" I asked Drew. He gave me the thumbs-up, even though he was looking kind of green. I choked back a laugh. I get that he was nervous about performing, but we were on the soccer field. His turf. Then again, I'd seen how he performed on this field before. He wasn't exactly the star that Eric was.

I chose not to point that out, particularly considering how our skit started.

Our emcee for the afternoon, Gary, got up on the now functioning mic and did a bit with the crowd, claiming it was the dialogue they missed from his earlier skit. The audience loved every second of it, though I could see Holly seething from where I was standing beside the stands.

Gary introduced our group, and I gave a nod to Drew. He nodded back, still green, but raring to go. He kicked the soccer ball to me and I took it out onto the field. Drew followed and we passed the ball back and forth like we were playing an actual game. I'm happy to say that I didn't trip over my own feet, kick the ball into the trees, or take out anyone in the crowd with the round projectile. It was just like it was back when Drew and I were kids playing together . . . oh so many years ago.

Once we reached the stage, we acted surprised to find the prop chalice sitting there. I'd argued earlier that we needed to come up with an explanation for it being there, but Hope told me I was over-thinking and I was voted down.

Drew picked up the chalice to the sound of thunder effects courtesy of a metal sheet Marq was working backstage that we'd borrowed from the prop shed. As long as the headmaster didn't see Marq helping, we figured we could bend the rules a bit.

At the sound of thunder, Drew and I jumped to signify we had traveled back in time. (Hey, we were going low budget here. The thunder was as special as these effects were going to get. Go with it.) As we took in our new surroundings— marked by a tree Hope slid from one side of the stage to the other, Sam and Suze came up in their Renaissance costumes and stumbled across us.

"What strange manner of man is this?" Sam asked. "In such odd vestments."

Drew and I shared an exaggerated look of confusion and he turned to the girls and said the line I had begged him not to say. "We come in peace."

Oddly, the audience cracked up over his line and we were off and running.

Fish-out-of-water high jinks ensued while Drew and I tried to figure out what was going on and how to communicate with Sam and Suze . . . well, mostly Sam because Suze wasn't up to date on all her Renaissance slang. We had them rolling in the stands by the time Hope stomped onstage in her executioner's robes condemning us to death because she caught us in our nonconformist clothing. (A little social satire on our part that we suspected most of the audience wouldn't get. And we were right. I remind you that I'd previously changed into Eric's Abercrombie & Fitch shirt.)

The roar from the crowd was deafening as Hope chased us around the stage swinging her executioner's axe. It was quickly drowned out by the gasps when the trick axe connected with Drew's neck and appeared to go clean through. When Drew paused to make sure his head remained attached, the audience went wild with applause.

Hope renewed her attack, trapping all four of us at the corner of the stage. Just as she switched to her much, *much* bigger axe, Eric stepped onto the stage and I swear we had a minor earthquake. The audience went *insane*. They were laughing, cheering, making wolfcalls in his direction. Naturally, Eric was eating it up. That ham.

I have to admit, he did make a lovely girl, what with his disgustingly smooth skin and fair features. Suze had even managed to corset his manly chest into an impressive rack. So long as he didn't turn his back to the audience—revealing that we couldn't quite lace him up all the way since he's somewhat broader than Marq—he made the perfect queen.

Until he opened his mouth. The audience went wild over his exaggerated falsetto, but it was nothing like the truly believable performance Marq had put on the first day we'd met.

The day was saved. We took our bows to a standing ova-
tion and basked in the love. Sound problems or not, we *rocked*
our skit in so many ways that Holly's did not. We regrouped
backstage, basking in the post-skit buzz and recapping every
second of the performance. Drew and Eric were more excited
than anyone, with Eric actually commenting that he felt
better than he did when he scored a goal in soccer.

High praise, indeed.

Sam finally got us all down to a dull roar so she could
speak. I could feel the emotion coming off her in waves. "I just
want to thank you guys," she said. "Aside from shoving our
skit in Holly's face, which was fun . . . I always hoped you
guys would get along," Sam continued. "But I never . . ." At
that point, she got all choked up and couldn't talk. Eric, to his
immense credit, wrapped her up in his arms and gave her a
serious kiss, making sure his makeup rubbed all over her face.

"I figured this is the only chance I'd have to kiss a girl while
I'm the one in lipstick," he said when they finally broke apart.

"Honey," Marq said, taking Eric's face between his thumb
and his forefinger, squeezing it to the point that his lips puckered again. "Never say never!"

"Let's go have some fun!" Sam said, grabbing Marq by the
arm (for a change) and pulling him away from Eric and out to
meet the rest of her school friends.

"Wait!" I said. I wasn't done with Marq yet, but before he
got lost in the crowd, he managed to throw me what I'd asked
him to get.

We were mobbed. *Everyone* came out of the stands to

congratulate us. And as awesome as that was, it was *nothing* compared to the feeling when I saw Holly standing off to the side with Alexis and Belinda waiting for someone—anyone— to come up and compliment her. Well, her dad was there, but that was to be expected.

The star of the afternoon turned out to be Eric. No surprise there. He tends to be a star wherever he goes and whatever he does. The difference this time is that he was basking in the stardom totally in drag. He was enjoying the attention so much that he either forgot to change out of his dress or decided that it was simply more fun to keep it on, but he stayed in his outfit for the rest of the afternoon.

Several times over the course of the day, I tried to pull Sam aside, but she was too busy trying to drain every last second of Marq Time before he left. I'd almost forgotten that he was heading up to San Francisco first thing in the morning Tuesday. At least now he'd be stationary and a lot closer than he'd been while traveling the globe with the Renaissance Faire.

I sensed a road trip in our future.

It wasn't until late in the afternoon that I was able to take Sam away from everyone for a quiet moment behind the bleachers. No. Not like that. Although, we weren't the only ones sneaking behind the bleachers.

"My eyes! My eyes!" I shouted as we stumbled into Hope and Drea sharing a clandestine kiss.

"Oh, grow up!" Hope said. "We were just saying good-bye." I guess we spoiled the moment because they stormed off, holding hands.

Sam looked at me with a raised eyebrow.

"It is what it is," I said . . . with a shrug.

"So, what's going on?" she asked. "Marq's leaving soon. I don't want to—"

"I know," I said, "but I've been trying to give you something all day."

"Grief?" she joked.

"Ha. Ha." I said, then thrust something into her hands. "This."

She held the silver chain up in the sunlight to get a better look. A silver dragonfly was suspended in the air between us.

"It's beautiful," she said.

"A Florella original," I replied. "I asked Marq to swing by and pick it up this morning."

"Oh, Bryan," she said with a sigh while undoing the clasp. "What's it for?"

"It's because I'm tired of looking at your naked neck," I said. "Now you can wear that every day . . . or every few days . . . or just hang it in your locker and look at it when you feel down. I don't care. And don't go attaching any legendary mythology to it. I just got it as a symbol of our friendship. It doesn't mean anything more than that."

She clipped the clasp behind her neck and let the dragonfly lie against her skin. "I wouldn't be too sure about that." She gave me a friendly kiss on the cheek to thank me before we rejoined our friends.

Okay, so I kind of lied about the symbol thing. After I talked to Marq on the beach about getting Sam a necklace, I went home and researched some stuff online. According to this one site I found, the dragonfly symbolized "moving past self-created illusions that limit our ability to grow and change." I immediately called Marq and told him that's what I wanted. It was perfect in this situation, for a number of reasons. But Sam didn't need to know any of that. All I wanted her to focus on was that it looked pretty. Which it did.

When we returned from behind the bleachers, Marq was going all, "Oooooooo," trying to imply that we'd been up to no good. Considering that all Eric did was laugh at that, I'm guessing he didn't feel too threatened by our brief disappearance.

The light moment was broken up when Marq started looking all sad. "Sammy, I've got to get back to the faire and help my folks start packing up. We've got a lot of things to ship north tomorrow morning."

Tears were welling up in Sam's eyes. And I have to admit, I was feeling kind of moved myself. Marq lightened the mood by pulling Sam into an enormous hug, dipping her back, and giving her a prolonged kiss good-bye. I mean, minutes passed. Eric was starting to look uncomfortable even though there was nothing at all to be jealous about.

Finally, the kiss came to an end.

"Wow," Sam said. "My toes curled on that one."

"Sorry, dude," Marq said to Eric as he went in for an embrace.

Much like I did when I'd first met Marq, Eric shoved his hand between them before things got a bit too friendly. Marq shook hands with Eric and Drew while trading off good-byes with Drea. He gave Hope and Suze each kisses good-bye.

Then . . . he turned to me with arms open wide.

What the hell, I thought as I let him wrap me up in a hug and give me a friendly kiss on the lips in front of my closest friends.

I didn't even worry about the sound of the click that came from the camera phone I saw Alexis slipping into her pocket when we were done. Not that she was going to raise anyone's interest level by passing that image around to the gossip sites, since no one would have a clue who I was.

But, I sensed a mass e-mail to the student mailing list was definitely in my future.

Which didn't bother me at all.

And . . . scene.

Renaissance Faire Glossary

Here's a little primer to help figure out what the heck everyone is talking about. I only wish I'd had it before I'd gone to the faire.

ALACKADAY: darn

ANON: soon

APOTHECARY: pharmacy/drugstore

AYE: yes

BEMADDING: maddening

CHATMATES: close friends

CLUMPERTON: silly fellow

CODPIECE: decorative pouch attached to the front of men's breeches

COUSIN: a close friend

DOXY: a beggar's wench or a prostitute

FARTHING: old coin equal to one fourth of a British penny

FIE: expression of annoyance or disgust

FLIBBERTIGIBBET: gossip; silly, flighty person

GOD A MERCY: God have mercy

GOD'S TEETH: geez

GOODMAN: the man of the house

GOOD MORROW: good morning

GOODWIFE: the woman of the house

GORBELLIED: having a potbelly

GULL: fool

HAGSEED: the child of a hag

HOW NOW?: How are you?

HUZZAH: hooray

IN GOOD SOOTH: honestly

KNAVE: a man of low social position; servant

LACED MUTTON: prostitute

LAYABOUT LOUT: lazy person

LIGHTSKIRT: woman of easy virtue

MARRY: wow

MAYHAP: maybe

MILKSOP: wimp

MOONLING: simpleton

NAY: no

PRITHEE: pray thee; please

SWAG: blustery man

THITHER: there

WELL-MET: good to see you

WENCH: a girl, usually from the peasant class

YON: something a distance away, but still within sight

There's always more  Look for:

★ *Entrances and Exits* ★

It's time for the Fall One-Act Festival, and Hope gets the honored privilege of debuting her very first original play! With Bryan directing and Jason and Sam as the leads, it seems like nothing could go wrong with this dream team of talent. But where's the fun in that?

Enter Sam and Jason's onstage chemistry that's so hot, it's working overtime offstage! Course, Sam's real-life beau, Eric, isn't so cool with that. And what about Bryan? With our fabulous narrator's sexual orientation now public knowledge, he's gaining some admiring attention from the most unexpected places. Can you blame them?

With all these raging hormones, it'll be a wonder if the play goes off at all. And the afterparty? Please—that'll be a show all in itself. . . .

About the Author

Paul Ruditis has never worn a costume to a Renaissance Faire, a Revolutionary War reenactment, or a *Star Trek* convention, though he has been to each of those events . . . on more than one occasion. *Show, Don't Tell* is the third book in the DRAMA! series, following *The Four Dorothys* and *Everyone's a Critic*. Visit him online at www.paulruditis.com.